A Scottie Ramone Cozy Mystery

CAUGHT Bread HANDED

LONDON LOVETT

one
. . .

A NEW SPRING sun winked at us from the eastern sky as Jack and I finished stacking warm loaves of bread in the baskets. Those same loaves filled my sparkling, new bakery with the sweet aroma that only freshly baked bread could produce. Outside the front window, pinkish, wispy clouds held the promise of a nice spring morning. The days were getting longer, but warmer temperatures were still a month off for those of us living in the Rockies. And our little town of Ripple Creek always seemed to be farthest behind on the winter thaw. A river ran through town, its icy banks and frothy snow melt keeping a chill in the air. We were also surrounded by tall peaks on three sides, shrouding us in cool shadows much of the time.

"Ahh, the life of a baker," Jack said. "What other profession gets to experience so many sunrises?" Jack Lucas had turned up at my bakery door at a time when I was in desperate need of an assistant. He was in his sixties, with scruffy gray hair and a naval tattoo on his meaty forearm. He looked more like a grizzly bear crossed with a lumberjack than a baker's assistant. His gruff appearance and troubled past had almost kept me from hiring him, but the man was a magician with bread dough. He could bake a sponge so light it practically floated off the plate, and he could decorate a cake fit for a royal wedding. He was reliable and hardworking and a great companion in the shop. It had been my lucky day when Jack walked into the shop, and I told him that every chance I got.

"Sunrises are one of the perks of the job. Although the flipside of that is dragging yourself out of a warm bed while it's still dark outside and the entire landscape is covered in frost." I pulled a stack of napkins and paper bags out from under the counter. Soon, a parade of regulars would line up at the counter of Scottie's Bakery to buy their usual morning pastries or muffins.

My dream of owning a bakery had come true. It had taken persistence and jumping over many obstacles to get here (including ditching a controlling fiancé), but it had been worth every hurdle and headache. After training in Paris, I'd landed a high-caliber job in a fancy restaurant, but I'd always kept my dream alive. A dramatic incident brought me back to my hometown of Ripple Creek, a place where nature met you at every corner and community meant more than anything. My grandmother, Evie, or Nana as I called her, had raised me after the tragic death of my parents. Now she'd welcomed me back into her life with open arms. In fact, the entire town was glad to have me back, and I was thrilled to repay them for all their love and support by providing them with delicious baked goods.

A timer rang in the back. Jack placed the last loaf of sourdough in the basket. "That'll be the brownies. I'll pull them out."

I walked across to the front door and flipped the sign to open. The rush would start shortly. Along with their morning treat, customers liked to grab a fresh loaf of bread before we sold out. I was just circling back behind the counter when the door opened. It was my first customer of the day and a person I never got tired of seeing. My unexpected return to Ripple Creek had thrown my childhood crush back into my path. I'd spent many of my younger years dreaming that one day I'd marry Dalton Braddock. But he moved away when we were in our early teens, and a piece of my heart left with him. It took many tears, love songs on the radio and dozens of Nana's oatmeal cookies for me to finally accept that I'd never see Dalton again. Then, suddenly there he was. I returned to Ripple Creek to discover that he'd become ranger for both the town and the resort above it. He was still as breath-stealing as ever, but he was also very much attached to Crystal Miramont of the Miramont Resort family. Growing up, Dalton had been one of my favorite people. At the same time, Crystal had been one of my least favorites. I was well into adulthood now, but those designations hadn't changed.

"Good morning, Ranger Braddock. What can I get you this morning?"

Dalton's big, expensive wedding was just a few months away, but he never liked to talk about it. The topic could even make him grumpy. I assumed it was pre-wedding jitters. I, myself, had been heading to a lavish wedding, planned mostly by a pushy mother-in-law-to-be, but coming back to Ripple Creek had made me realize I wasn't happy in my relationship. Those jitters jumped me right out of the wedding just days before the big event.

Dalton was tall with broad shoulders. I could swear they'd been broad even in middle school. His brown eyes sparkled as he stared at the pastries behind the glass. "I would just like to point out that I've had to move my belt over a notch since this bakery opened, Scottie."

"And yet, here you are, trying to decide between a cheese and an apricot Danish. May I suggest both?" I smiled teasingly.

"Oh, you're good, you're real good. But since 'self-control' is my middle name, I'll stick with one—the cheese, please."

"Good choice." I picked up the tongs and slid open the case. The smell of sugar glaze wafted out. "I don't think you should blame your belt issues on my light and airy pastries. I'd blame those mocha lattes with the whipped cream."

Dalton laughed. "You're probably right. I'm off those right now." He didn't elaborate, but his expression told me it had something to do with a tuxedo fitting for the topic that-should-not-be-named.

I decided not to press him about mocha lattes.

Jack came out from the back. "Ranger Braddock. First customer of the day, I see."

"Yep. I was out on patrol, and I'm embarrassed to admit, I drove past the shop twice waiting to see the sign flip." Dalton had been adamantly against me hiring Jack as my assistant. He knew Jack's history and tried hard to convince me to look elsewhere. It had been a source of contention between us. It turned out I'd been right, and Dalton now saw it was a good decision. It had taken a month or two for the ice to break between the two men, but they were officially on friendly terms, and I was relieved.

I dropped the pastry into a bag along with a napkin. "How's it going out there? Bringing all the bad guys to justice?"

"Well, if you count the three raccoons that found their way into Francine Cocoran's basement as bad guys, then yes, they've been brought to justice. I scared them out of the house and helped secure the basement vent."

"Sounds like a good plot for a movie," Jack quipped. "And here's a better one," he added under his breath so that only I caught the words.

The door opened and Cade Rafferty walked in. He was wearing a forest green sweater that complimented his light hazel eyes. He could compete with Dalton for height and shoulder breadth. While Dalton was a more down-to-earth, rugged type, Cade was elegant and undeniably dashing. Dalton looked like he could be the hero in an action-adventure movie, whereas Cade looked as if he would be entirely comfortable playing the part of a love-interest in a Jane Austen remake. Cade, a successful author of gothic thrillers, had moved into his ancestor's estate just a few miles from town. It was a rundown manor house with an overgrown set of gardens, but he was slowly bringing the estate back to its glory days. We became instant friends. Sometimes, it seemed we were tiptoeing around being more than friends.

Dalton glanced back to see who'd walked in. Their gazes clashed. I could almost hear the buzzing sound of two light sabers colliding. To say that Dalton and Cade were not friends was an understatement. The two men had taken an instant disliking to each other, and while Dalton and Cade (who had also advised against hiring Jack but in a much less bossy way) had both come to like Jack, they'd never learned to like each other.

You could feel a chill in the air as they passed, Dalton on his way out and Cade on his way in. Cade glanced back to watch Dalton leave, then turned around and slammed, metaphorically speaking, into my look of displeasure.

"Uh oh, did I forget a birthday?" he asked facetiously.

"You know exactly why I'm wearing this annoyed expression."

Cade shrugged. "It's his fault."

"How is it only his fault?" I asked.

"He's interminably unlikable."

"Never mind," I said with exasperation. I'd tried more than once to mend the rift between them, but I'd found it was a waste of time and energy. "What can I get you, Mr. Rafferty?"

Cade's brows bunched in a frown. "The only other person who ever called me that in such a scolding tone was my fifth-grade teacher, Mrs. Crone, a woman who wore a permanent glower. For some odd reason she always had black cats following her around."

"Is that true?" Jack asked. He didn't know Cade as well as I did.

I shook my head. "Don't forget, Mr. Rafferty is a master of fiction." I turned back to Cade. "And now that you've compared me to an old witch, what can I get you from my glass case. May I suggest the prune Danish or bran muffin?"

Jack laughed.

"And to think I shaved and everything for my trip to the bakery." Cade rubbed his smooth chin.

I could never stay mad at him long. "Well, since you shaved, I suppose you'll want your usual, an apricot Danish? They're fresh out of the cauldron." I winked.

"Seems I should go back to bed and try getting out on the other side. No bag. I'll eat it on the way home."

I handed him the Danish and our fingers touched. Warmth and a trace of electricity was exchanged. Our gazes held for a long moment, then the door opened. Customers were arriving, and the morning rush was about to begin.

"Later, Ramone." Cade took a bite of his Danish as he walked out of the store.

"I just hope it doesn't come to a duel between those two," Jack muttered before moving to the counter to help a customer.

two
. . .

AFTER THE SOMEWHAT ABRASIVE start to the day, the rest of the morning slid by gracefully. Cade sent me multiple texts to apologize and let me know that he was a tiresome scallywag and a court jester with few good jests and that he couldn't understand why I kept him in my social circle. I laughed as I wrote back that his preceding texts were exactly why I kept him in my social circle. Life would be dull without him.

    Jack leaned into the display cabinets to move pastries together so there weren't so many blank spots on the trays. "Looks like cheese was the winner this morning," he said as he backed his wide shoulders out of the glass case and straightened. "And apple was the loser. Maybe we should increase the cheese by a dozen and decrease the apple by the same amount."

"Good idea. Now that fall is long past, people are no longer interested in apple pastries." I pulled out a notepad from my apron and wrote it down. "We should be getting those fresh strawberries in the next produce order, then we can take out the apple altogether and make fresh strawberry tarts."

Jack tightened his apron. "I'm going to start on tomorrow's cinnamon rolls." Jack and I found out early on that our menu was too varied and offered far too many choices for us to keep up with the baking. Cinnamon rolls were a town favorite, but making them every day along with the pastries was too much, so we made Friday cinnamon roll day. We generally made far fewer pastries that day because our loyal customers lined up for cinnamon rolls. Jack made a superb cream cheese frosting for the rolls, which made them an extra big hit.

The door opened and two regular customers walked in. Rusty Simmer was a retired travel agent. He had a thick head of gray hair, and he walked slightly hunched over. You could always count on Rusty to have a pair of reading glasses on a chain around his neck, and you could always expect him to be smiling. This morning was no different as he gazed at the pastries in front of him. His friend Cameron Burke was about the same age—seventy-something—but had a much sturdier build. He did, however, walk with a profound limp. He broke his knee skiing ten years earlier. He always wore sweater vests over short-sleeved dress shirts and, because he was an avid coin collector, he always kept a magnifying glass in his pocket. Rusty collected coins as well. Both men also spent a lot of time at the chess tables in the park.

"Rusty, Cameron, you two are late. I guess it was too cold for chess in the park this morning."

Rusty's grin lit up his face. "We'll still be playing chess today. Heading over there after we order cookies for our coin club meeting."

"Cookies? Great. Let me get an order form, and we can mark off what kind you need." I walked to the cash register and pulled an order form out of the drawer. "When will you need these?"

Both men winced. Cameron spoke up hesitantly. "Tomorrow evening? I know it's late notice, but Rusty was supposed to remind me."

Rusty turned to him. "You were in charge of refreshments this month. I hardly see how it can be my fault."

"Because on Monday, when we were playing a game of chess, I said to you—I said—'Rusty, remind me to order a tray of cookies from the bakery for Friday's meeting.' Apparently, you're not someone I can count on for reminders."

Rusty rolled his eyes. "Next time buy yourself a pad of those sticky notes and plaster one to your forehead. Then you'll remember." Rusty turned back to me. "If it's too late, Scottie, that's all right. We can buy some boxed cookies at the market."

"Nonsense, I wouldn't hear of it. It's not too late." I handed them the order sheet and a pen. "Check off which kinds you want and how many of each, and we'll have the tray ready for your meeting."

"See, I told you Scottie wouldn't let us down," Cameron said.

The windows on the bakery rattled, and we all turned toward the loud truck outside. It was an old Chevy. The bed was piled high with old furniture.

"Who on earth?" Rusty laughed. "I've got a sudden urge to sing the Beverly Hillbillies' theme song."

"That's Henry Voight's old truck," Cameron said. "I'd recognize it anywhere, only he usually has gardening tools in the back, not furniture."

"Maybe he's moving," Rusty suggested. "Looks like we're about to find out. He's coming into the bakery."

Henry Voight was a fifty-something landscaper married to a nurse named Arlene. The couple owned a century-old bungalow just south of town. They'd been restoring it forever. Arlene came into the bakery occasionally for a loaf of bread, but she rarely bought sweets because she complained that Henry ate far too much rich food. And Arlene might have been right about that. Henry's belly had grown a bit since the last time I saw him. His wispy blond hair was thinner, too.

"Henry, you moving out of town?" Cameron asked.

"Me? After all the money and time we put into that house?" Henry chuckled. "We're never going to leave that place."

"What's with all the furniture?" Rusty asked.

"Oh, that. Well, Arlene's been bugging me to clear out the basement. She's got some grand plans to make it a cozy living space." Henry shook his head. "I told her basements and cozy don't go together, but once she sets her mind on something, I just smile and nod. No sense debating her. That stuff was left behind by Marvin, the past owner of the house."

Rusty walked to the window and stretched up from his usual hunched posture to get a view of the items in the truck. "Looks like you've got a few antiques in there."

"That's what Arlene said too. I don't know much about furniture, but some of it is quality-made, unlike the stuff they're passing off as furniture nowadays. I sent some photos to Amy at the antique shop, and she said to pile it in the truck and bring it to the store. She's going to make an offer once she's looked everything over."

I was eyeing the old bookshelf at the back of the truck. Cade had been hunting for a set of solid wood bookshelves.

Henry came up to the counter. He stared longingly at the pastries. "That apricot Danish sure looks good."

"Would you like it?" I asked as I picked up the tongs.

"Gosh, I shouldn't. Arlene has this sixth sense when it comes to me sneaking treats. I guess I'm not good at hiding guilt. She texted me as I left the house and said I needed to stop by the bakery first to buy a loaf of multi-seeded sourdough. She even makes me eat healthy bread."

"That's because she loves you," I told him. "And you're in luck, I still have a multi-seeded sourdough in the basket." I pulled on a latex glove, grabbed the last seeded sourdough and put it in a bag. I rang him up. "Good luck with the furniture appraisal."

Henry walked out. The windows vibrated as his old truck fired up and waddled down the road with its heavy load. After some debate and a few insults about taste in cookies,

Cameron and Rusty picked their cookie assortment, bought a few pastries and left.

For the first time since I'd flipped the sign this morning, the shop was empty. But a baker's work was never done. The cookie tray was not on the schedule, so I had to start baking right away. Fortunately, I had an amazing assistant to help.

three
...

FOR THE FIRST FEW MONTHS, Jack and I were so busy in the shop, we never took proper lunch breaks. After a particularly busy morning and one cupcake-burning disaster, we both sat down with aching backs and flour-streaked faces. That was when we decided to pare down the daily offerings and made a pact to always take a lunch break. It was a small town and local shop owners often closed for lunch. The bakery officially closed at two, so instead of shutting down for lunch, we staggered our breaks. We both always made a point of leaving the bakery for the break. It was too easy to pull out a sandwich, only to be dragged out to the front of the shop by an unexpected rush of customers. Nana's house was only a five-minute drive from the bakery, which gave me a nice, mind-settling lunch option.

Nana was out filling the birdfeeders as I pulled up. It was the time of year when all the wonderful migrators came through and thrilled us with their brief visits. Popsicle-colored tanagers and lemon-yellow orioles were sitting on nearby fence posts, waiting for Nana to pop orange slices onto the ends of the feeders.

"Button, I made you an egg salad sandwich and some homemade lemonade." Nana finished with the orange slices. "All right, you guys, have at it." As if they understood her, two orioles dove toward the orange slices. Nana was in her eighties, but she still had the spunk and energy of someone in their twenties. Occasionally, I'd catch her pressing a hand to her lower back or stretching her fingers to relieve some arthritis, but then I was in my early forties and I did the same. My parents, a highly-successful couple, had left me behind with a nanny while they went skiing in the Alps. I was only seven when they were both swept to their deaths in an avalanche. My mom had not always gotten along with her mom. They had different ideas on how to live a good life. Fortunately, my mom had made certain that Nana would raise me if something ever happened to both my parents. And so, at that early age, I left my parents' expensive penthouse and moved into Nana's tiny cabin in the woods. She helped me heal from the tragedy by providing a never-ending stream of love.

I took Nana's arm, and we headed inside. We were met with the sound of coins clinking against each other. Nana's neighbor and good friend, Hannah, was on the couch, bent over a pile of coins on the coffee table. She used a magnifying glass to get a closer look at each coin.

"Are you ladies planning a trip to Las Vegas?" I asked.

"Hannah's looking through all those old coins to see if she can find anything of value," Nana explained.

Hannah looked up from her task long enough to explain her sudden interest in old coins. "I decided I need to socialize more, so I joined the coin collectors club a few months back." She lifted a small paperback off the table. "Rusty lent me his collector's guide book. It's actually kind of fun. I feel like an archaeologist, only instead of old bones, I'm looking through old coins."

"And instead of sitting in the desert under the hot Egyptian sun, you're sitting on my couch in front of the fireplace," Nana added.

Hannah shrugged. "Not quite as adventurous but I personally think old bones are overrated."

Nana rubbed the knuckles on her hands. "I couldn't agree more. In fact, I'd like to trade my old bones in for some new ones. Do you want a sandwich, Hannah? Or are you too deep in your treasure hunt to step away?"

"Actually, I'm hungry. I'll just go wash up."

I followed Nana into the kitchen. It smelled sharply of egg salad. "I just realized I'm starved," I said. "Sometimes being surrounded by wonderful smells all day can make you forget that you haven't eaten." I sat down in my favorite spot at the table. The chair had always wobbled a little. As a kid I used to rock back and forth on it as I ate my breakfast or did my homework. It also gave me a nice view of the front yard where a rainbow of little birds competed for the fresh oranges.

Hannah returned and Nana placed sandwiches and

lemonade down on the table.

"I hear you guys are having a coin meeting tomorrow," I said. "Rusty and Cameron came in to order some cookies for the meeting."

"Oh good, then there'll be yummy treats. Last month, June Farthington baked a pineapple upside-down cake, and I think that darn cake should have been left right-side up. It was a mess, and the cake was hard as a rock."

Nana laughed. "I remember when June baked cupcakes to sell at the street fair. Poor thing. I don't know if she sold even one cupcake. Is Cameron still the president of the club?"

Hannah rolled her eyes. "Yes, but he's self-appointed. No one wanted to run for the position, so Cameron took over. He and Rusty are always so darn competitive. Instead of just sharing anything interesting they've found, the two spend half the meeting debating whose find was the most valuable or the rarest. I've heard it's the same thing at the chess tables. They're friends one minute, and the next, they're angry at each other about a game of chess."

"Have you found anything interesting in that pile of coins?" Nana asked.

"A few old coins from the forties but nothing that we can both retire on," Hannah said with a laugh.

"This sandwich is delicious, Nana. I really needed this. I've still got a lot to do in the shop today."

Nana gave me her worried grandmother look. "Are you sure you're not working too hard?"

"Running a bakery is hard work, but I knew that going in. It's rewarding, hard work. And Jack is a great help."

"Oh, I ran into Jack at the market," Hannah said. "He's such a nice man. I couldn't reach a can of soup, and he took it down for me. Oh, speaking of nice men—how are Dalton and Cade?"

I covered my mouth to stop from laughing and spitting out food. "Smooth transition, Hannah. And I assume they're both fine." I decided to leave off this morning's near shoulder-clashing visit. Hannah and Nana were both aware of my decades-long crush on Dalton. They also both thought highly of Cade. His charisma was as smooth as butter. It was easy to like him, unless, of course, your name was Dalton Braddock. Nana and, seemingly, Jack, were convinced that Cade and Dalton's mutual dislike stemmed from their mutual fondness for a certain baker. I was always quick to remind everyone of Dalton's impending marriage to a stunningly beautiful, rich woman.

"Boy, that Crystal Miramont is an impolite—well, you know," Hannah said. "My dentist is up the hill, near the resort, and while I was up there, I decided to stop in one of the cute gift shops in the resort village." Hannah huffed. "A bunch of overpriced junk, I can tell you that. Crystal was there ordering special candles for her bridesmaids' gift bags. I stopped to introduce myself and let her know I was a good friend of Dalton's. She rudely put up a hand to stop me. Her pink fingernails must have been an inch long, and there were tiny rhinestones pasted on top."

I glanced down at my nails. They were short and broken, and my hands were raw and red from work and the repeated handwashing necessary when handling food.

"Anyhow, she immediately said—'I'm sorry but the guest list is complete. We don't have room to invite anyone else,'" Hannah continued. "Can you imagine the gall? She thought I was trying to get invited to her ridiculous wedding. All I wanted to do was say congratulations. Which I didn't. Not after that. I was so dumbstruck I didn't even respond. I just walked out of the store shaking my head. I worry about Dalton. He's going to be entering the lion's den with that family. They've always been rude and unlikable."

"He'll be perfectly happy," I said. I wasn't sure why I always felt the need to defend his marriage to Crystal. I suppose I just wanted Dalton to be happy. A long time ago I wanted that happiness to be with me, but I'd grown up and learned a lot about the world since then. Life doesn't always hand you a bowl of cherries. Sometimes you have to learn how to use the pits. My happily-ever-after with Dalton was never meant to be. My thirteen-year-old self would find that hard to accept, but the forty-year-old Scottie had come to terms with it. I was glad to move on, and I was happy for Dalton. I wasn't Crystal's biggest fan, but I was sure she'd make a good partner.

I finished my sandwich and leaned back with a satisfied groan. "Nana, that was exactly what I needed to finish my day."

Nana sat up straighter. "You aren't leaving already?"

"I've got to make cookies for the coin collectors' meeting. Good luck with your archaeological dig on the coffee table, Hannah. I hope you find something rare and valuable."

four
· · ·

JACK WAS in the kitchen washing pans. He clanged them around as if he was angry about something. The dish soap bubbles floating around the wash area seemed to indicate the same thing. His big shoulders were tense as he scrubbed a cake pan.

"Jack? Is something wrong?"

He looked over his shoulder and forced a smile. "I didn't hear you come in, Scottie." He turned off the water and dried his hands with a dishtowel. "Nothing's the matter. Just a bout of hurt feelings, that's all."

"What happened?"

Jack's big chest rounded with a deep breath. "I just need a tougher skin. I have to accept the fact that not everyone is Scottie Ramone. Not everyone can look past this—" He waved his hand in front of himself.

"Past what?" I took his hand. "Come sit down and I'll get you a glass of water."

He shook his head. "No, I'm fine. Washing the pans is making me feel better." He chuckled. "They might end up cleaner than when they were brand new." He returned to the sink, and I grabbed a dry towel to help.

After a few minutes of washing and drying, he finally spoke up. "It's that woman Dalton is marrying. I understand wanting someone beautiful and wealthy, but sometimes the price to pay for that is too high."

"You're talking about Crystal? Did she come into the bakery?"

"She sure did, but she crinkled her nose and face just like this." Jack turned his face my direction and scrunched it up tight. It was hard not to laugh because he looked so darn cute doing it. "She needed to order a cake for a wedding shower, but she refused to work with me. She said she'd wait to talk to you."

This time I did laugh. "Well then, she really did slight you because she absolutely hates me."

"I'm not surprised," he said with a teasing grin.

"Why are you not surprised?"

"I think you know."

I stared back at him, blinking in confusion. "I mean she hasn't liked me since our school days, but in my defense, she only liked people more suited to her social circle. I wasn't exactly part of that club."

"That's because all she has is money. You have all the qualities that make you an outstanding human, something she lacks." I'd never mentioned to Jack that I spent my first seven years in a multi-million-dollar penthouse with a nanny and full-time chef. The fortune left to me by my parents and later my paternal grandparents would make the Miramonts green with envy. Only Nana knew about my bank account. I'd used some of the money to build the bakery, but otherwise, it remained untouched and, frankly, unloved. Nana raised me to admire life and adventures more than money.

"Thank you, Jack. That is sweet to say. And don't worry about Crystal. I'd say you dodged a bullet not having to help her. With any luck, she's ordered a cake from a different bakery, and we won't have to deal with her at all." My words should have been followed with three knocks on wood. The front door opened and Crystal walked in. Dalton stepped in after her looking as if he'd been dragged to the bakery against his will.

"Oh, good, you're back." Crystal pulled off her leather gloves and shoved them into her Chanel bag. I couldn't help but notice how completely mismatched they were as a couple. But then, supposedly, opposites attract. Maybe that had been my whole problem all along. I was too much like Dalton. We loved the same things, the same foods, the same jokes made us laugh. Heck, we even wore the same brand of hiking boots. The fact that I couldn't hold a candle to Crystal in the figure and beauty department probably had something to do with it too.

Jack had popped his head out to see if he was needed up front. He yanked his head back and disappeared like a prairie dog spotting a coyote or, in this case, a leather coated, diamond-bedecked mountain lion.

"I need to order a cake for a wedding shower."

Dalton looked at her confused. "Wait, didn't you just have a wedding shower last week?"

Crystal laughed. It was as fake as her nails. She leaned over and made a show of kissing him. "Oh sweetie, that was for my mom's side of the family. This one is for my dad's family."

"Why didn't you just have them together?" he asked. It seemed she'd talked him into a trip to the bakery but hadn't mentioned the reason.

Another almost comically fake laugh. "Sweetie, you know they can't stand each other."

"Should make for an interesting reception," Dalton muttered. Crystal ignored the comment.

"I need you to make a Lady Baltimore cake." She said it in a way that reminded everyone she rarely heard the word *no*.

Dalton wasn't having it. "Crys, that sounded like a command." He looked at me apologetically, and as our gazes caught, there was something else in the way he looked at me. It almost seemed like homesickness, like he was wishing for something that he missed. "Do you make Lady Baltimore cakes?" he asked, politely.

Crystal didn't give me time to answer (no I don't). "Of course, she knows how. She's a trained baker. They all know how."

The Lady Baltimore cake was technically a fictional cake from a famous novel. It was a white cake with a boozy fruit and nut filling and mounds of fluffy meringue frosting. "Well, if I'd been trained in the South where they are popular, I might know how. But I was trained in Paris." That comment made her flinch.

"Right, *Paris*." There was no way to miss the sarcasm in her tone. It seemed she didn't believe me, and that was fine. I still had no idea how to make a Lady Baltimore cake. If it had been anyone else asking, I would have made the effort to find a good recipe and create the cake, but I wasn't in the mood to do it for Crystal.

"I just assumed all bakers knew how to make them," Crystal said. "My grandmother would like to have one at the party. I guess I'll have to try another baker."

"I know how to make one," Jack said from behind.

Crystal's nostrils flared, and her lip twitched.

I smiled at her. "There you go. It seems that we can fill your order, after all."

Crystal stood still at the counter, her spiky heels tapping occasionally on the floor. Dalton knew exactly why she was hesitating, and again, he wasn't having it. "Perfect, Jack, thanks so much. Next Saturday, right, *sweetie*?" Dalton used her favorite nickname back on her, but nothing about the way he said it was sweet.

Crystal fidgeted with her expensive purse. "Well, yes, but if you can't have it by then, I can go elsewhere."

"Saturday is not a problem," Jack said. "For how many guests?" I could have hugged him right then. He was confident and polite, and he was showing Crystal Miramont that he had way more class than her.

"Uh, fifty, please. And no almonds. My aunt is allergic."

"I use walnuts, but I'll make sure there's nothing in the kitchen with almond at that time that might cross-contaminate the cake." Jack pulled out his notepad and wrote down that important detail. He'd been so hurt by her attitude, but he was a true pro.

"Fine then. Should I leave a deposit?" Crystal asked as she lifted her purse.

"That's all right," I said. "After all, we're old school chums." I winked and it seemed to irritate her. Dalton was holding back a grin. He nodded and shot me his own wink before they walked out.

I turned to Jack. "Have I told you just how lucky I was when you walked into my bakery looking for a job?"

Jack's smile was a little crooked, but it worked for him. "Almost every day, but I never get tired of hearing it."

five
...

IT HAD BEEN ANOTHER SUCCESSFUL, though somewhat trying, day at the bakery. Jack went home, and I finished cleaning up. There was a knock on the front door. I poked my head out of the kitchen, ready to tell the person that we were closed for the day. It was Cade. He was holding a piece of cardboard. The words "Are we still friends?" were written in black marker. He moved to the next piece of cardboard. "Dinner at my place to make up for my roguish behavior?"

I laughed all the way to the door. "Someone's been watching too many Christmas rom-coms. Come on in. I'm just finishing up." He followed me to the kitchen. "And you being a master wordsmith, I'd like to point out your misuse of the word *roguish*." I reached around and pulled off my apron. "That implies someone who was acting mischievous in a playful way. I think churlish, grumpy, sullen would have been better choices."

"Ouch." He folded up his piece of cardboard. "But you're right, and I'm glad you're still talking to me after my boorish twin came in here this morning pretending to be me. I apologize for his behavior. Now how about dinner? I'll make macaroni and cheese and not from a box, I promise."

"I don't think I can turn down an offer like that. Did you get my message about the bookshelves? We could go to the antique store right now. I'm finished here for the day."

"You do put in long hours, Ramone. And you're loving it, aren't you?" he asked.

"I really am. Did you walk here? I've got my car."

"I did walk, and I'd like to go look at the bookshelves. Not exactly sure what I'm looking for, but it's not any of those fake wood, modern monstrosities I've been seeing online."

I pulled on my coat and grabbed my purse and keys. Ten minutes later, we were pulling up to Amy's Antiques. Amy Dency had restored an old cabin just off the highway and turned it into an antique shop. It was a favorite stop for people driving up to the resort, so she did great business. We'd arrived just an hour before closing and on a Thursday so there was only one other car in the small parking lot.

Amy's cat, an orange tabby named Spencer, was curled up on the front counter. Cade stopped to scratch the cat behind the ear. "I've been thinking about getting a pet. It's lonely in that big house." He sneezed. "I just remembered why I can't have a cat. Maybe a mini horse or a goat."

I laughed. "To live in the house?"

"Sure, why not? I've seen a video of Arnold

Schwarzenegger feeding his mini horse and donkey oatmeal cookies at the kitchen table."

"Maybe start with a parakeet or goldfish before jumping into farm animals."

Amy came out from the back room holding a stack of old books. She was around my age with dark brown hair and a flawless complexion. She loved to wear vintage dresses and hats in the summer when the crowds were big and the weather allowed for flowy cotton dresses. Since spring weather was still a month off, she was wearing jeans and a sweater. "Scottie, Cade, good to see you. I just got in a lot of cool stuff. Henry Voight was cleaning out his basement. Rusty Simmer is back there right now checking it all out."

"Yes, Rusty was in the bakery when Henry stopped by. Henry's Chevy was piled high with goodies," I explained. "Cade is here to see the bookshelves."

"Yes, there's a lovely pair of bookshelves. I can't date them, but I'd say turn-of-the-century. They're mahogany."

"Sounds promising," Cade said.

"I apologize for the clutter back there. I haven't had time to organize the new pieces, and since they came from a basement, they're quite dusty."

We made our way past a lovely Victorian dining set and found a rather disheveled pile of things in the back corner. Rusty was wearing his glasses. He glanced up over the top rims and smiled. "Scottie, Mr. Rafferty, good to see you."

"Please, call me Cade." Cade stepped over an ottoman with carved walnut legs. The upholstery was ripped and faded, but the base looked sturdy. I circled around an old sideboard that was thick with dust.

The bookshelves were the tallest items, so they were easy to find. Rusty busied himself with some of the smaller items: a silver teapot, a carved eagle and some old cigar boxes.

"Looking for anything special?" I asked Rusty.

He chuckled. "You know me—always looking for that elusive coin. I do love to browse through antiques. Makes me nostalgic for the old days."

I scoffed. "Now, you're not that old Rusty. This stuff was from before your time, too."

He nodded. "True. I'd say it's turn-of-the-century. What do you think of those shelves, Cade? Will they work in that grand old manor of yours?"

Cade took hold of one and gave it a little shake. It kept wobbling long after he released it. "Not sure. They're nice but not very sturdy."

"Nothing a little hammer and nails won't fix," Rusty said and returned to the stack of cigar boxes.

I joined Cade. He stepped back and tilted his head. "They're a little lopsided."

"Like Rusty said—nothing that a hammer and nails can't fix."

Cade looked behind him and then looked at me and pointed at his chest. "Oh, you were talking to me. I thought you were talking to someone with a toolbelt." He held up his long hands. "These fingers were meant for a keyboard. A hammer? Not so much. And my aversion to wielding a hammer all stems from a terrifying experience when I was ten. Let's just say, I lost a thumbnail and vowed never to touch one of those vile tools again."

I laughed and glanced over at Rusty to see if he'd heard the story. He was just snapping shut the lid on a cigar box. His face had taken on an ashen tone. He jammed the cigar box under his arm.

"Everything all right, Rusty?" I asked. "You look a little pale."

"Huh?" His face shot our direction as if he'd forgotten we were there. "Yes, yes, I'm fine."

"Looks like you found a cigar box you liked," I pointed out.

"Yes," he muttered. He hurried off without even saying goodbye. He grabbed a few things, randomly, an old book, a small vase and a wooden pull toy, then headed to the counter.

I looked at Cade. He raised a questioning brow.

"Did that seem strange to you?" I asked.

"Very." He returned his attention to the bookshelves. I leaned past a tall umbrella stand to get a glimpse of Rusty at the counter. He was talking animatedly to Amy about the pull toy, something about having one that was shaped like a horse when he was a boy. Nothing about his tone or the lively way he spoke seemed genuine, and I'd never seen Rusty act like anything but himself. He was trying to divert Amy's attention away from something. Even from my vantage point, I sensed it was the cigar box. He placed it on the counter almost as an afterthought, and he kept his hand on it. He didn't want her to open it.

"I think these are too far gone," Cade said.

I pulled my attention from the unusual scene at the counter. "That's too bad."

"Yes, the quest continues."

"There's a good cabinet builder down the hill. You could always have him make you a custom set of bookshelves."

"I like the way you think, Ramone. That might be the easiest way to get what I want." He gave one of the shelves a little shake. It creaked and leaned precariously to the side. "Oops, we should go."

I led the way. Rusty had finished paying. Declining a bag, he picked up all the items, taking special care to pick up the cigar box and tuck it safely under his arm. The other items probably had higher price tags, but with those he took no care at all. Cade hurried ahead to open the door for him. Rusty gave a quick nod and raced to his car.

"No luck with the shelves?" Amy asked.

"I don't think they're what I'm looking for," Cade said. "Thank you so much."

We stepped outside just in time to witness Rusty take off so fast his tires bounced as they hit the end of the parking lot.

"That man is making a clean getaway," Cade quipped.

"Sure looks like it. But getaway from what? I can't imagine there's a long list of people waiting to purchase one of those old cigar boxes." I watched as his car disappeared around the bend. It was odd behavior for Rusty, odd behavior indeed.

six
. . .

A HOT SHOWER and an hour of rest on Nana's couch and I was ready for dinner at Cade's. "You spend a lot of time with Cade." Nana was putting wood in the fireplace. The evenings were still brittle cold, and a warm fire was necessary.

"Do I? I guess I do. He's fun. There's never a dull moment with Cade. I won't be late. I've got an early start in the morning... again." It had taken a few months, but I'd finally gotten used to getting up in the dark. The early bakery hours meant I was usually asleep by eight. Tonight, I'd try to make it until nine. Cade understood. He said anyone who could drag themselves out of bed in the middle of the night deserved to hit the hay the second the moon showed up.

In the summer, it was easy to walk up the road and across the bridge to Cade's property. But the nights were still too cold and daylight too short to make that walk. I drove my car up his long gravel driveway and parked. I sat for a second trying to assess my feelings for the man inside the house. I'd spent an hour with him this afternoon, and I still looked forward to seeing him.

Whenever I saw Dalton, a group of butterflies did a little dance in my stomach. They weren't nearly as energetic as they used to be when I was a young girl and I saw Dalton standing in the schoolyard or at a party. Back then, they'd do more than a little dance. They'd perform a full-on trapeze act. I didn't get the butterflies with Cade, but I always looked forward to seeing him. I was sure I'd be sad if he left Ripple Creek or decided he didn't want to hang out anymore. Whenever we were together, my mind always raced with the possibility of that all-important first kiss. We'd come very close more than once. At one point, I was almost despondent about the lack of one, but Cade had diplomatically explained that he'd avoided that next step in our relationship because he sensed my heart was somewhere else, namely with Dalton. Cade had been married once, so caution was now in his nature. I had no idea how he knew about my crush on Dalton. It wasn't as if I walked around town with tiny Dalton stars in my eyes or his name doodled a million times and in a million ways on my school notebook. Still, Cade sensed there was something between Dalton and me and so, it seemed, Dalton was once again standing in the way of my happily ever after, only this time he was on the sidelines instead of center field. All of it left me befuddled and unsure of my feelings, Cade's feelings for me and everything in between.

Cade stepped through the front door. He was wearing a

black sweater over faded jeans and his thick hair curled up on his collar. His blinding white smile completed the picture.

I reached for the door handle. One thing was certain in my uncertain world; I was extremely glad that Cade had moved to town. I climbed out of the car. Daylight had evaporated enough that an uncomfortable chill had seeped into the air.

"Thought you might have changed your mind," Cade said.

"Once my belly has been told it's getting macaroni and cheese, there is no turning back." I reached the step he was standing on. For a second, I sensed metaphorical sparks between us as we gazed into each other's eyes.

Cade broke away from the electricity first. "Then, come on in. We don't want to keep your belly waiting." Cade helped me out of my coat. His hand brushed mine and stayed there for a second longer than necessary. I released the breath I'd been holding. He seemed to do the same.

There was no denying that sparks between us happened more often and with far more intensity each day. But still no butterflies. Was that a sign that the infatuation wasn't there, or was I just so programmed to act like a giddy teen around Dalton that those butterflies were doing their own thing? Why was my head always in such a muddle about this? Maybe it was because I wasted almost five years with Jonathan Rathbone, a man I was sure I loved, a man I was convinced would make me happy. I was wrong about all of it. Jonathan was merely a tall, successful prop in the middle of a play about my life, one I'd created to fit what I thought I wanted. I was sure a life with Jonathan would have made my parents happy and proud. But that life wasn't for me. Darn

Jonathan. Now I didn't trust my judgement when it came to men.

"Red or white?" Cade held up two bottles of wine. "Macaroni and cheese can go either way."

I laughed. "I think I'll stick with water. I have a four A.M. date with a blob of sourdough."

"You're much less fun now that sourdough has taken up so much of your time. I feel like I should be jealous of bread dough." He put away the wine and carried out a pitcher of ice water. "I knew you'd choose water. I added some lemon slices." He poured the chilled water into the wine glasses and handed me one.

"Very nice and thoughtful. Here's to macaroni and cheese and its very progressive attitude about wine." Our glasses touched along with our fingers. The sparks were back. Had the earlier incident in the bakery caused Cade to overcompensate with more emotion? Sometimes it just took an argument or uncomfortable moment to let two people know how much they cared about each other. He'd spent the whole morning apologizing. I doubted Dalton would have done the same if the arrival times had been switched and Dalton had been left behind in the bakery with a scowl and unkind comments. Or maybe I was underestimating Dalton. He'd certainly stepped in to defend Jack from Crystal's unkindness. (He probably had to do that a lot.)

"Have a seat and I'll pull out the mac and cheese. Help yourself to some salad."

I sat down at the table and served some salad in the bowls. Cade walked into the dining room holding two plates of macaroni and cheese. "I even added a breadcrumb topping," Cade said. "I'm becoming quite the chef."

"Gosh, yeah, Breadcrumb Topping 101 was my favorite class in the Paris culinary school," I teased. "But seriously, Cade, this looks delicious."

"Can't go too wrong with cheese and noodles." He sat down across from me. We enjoyed a few bites of food.

"I take back my earlier quip about the breadcrumbs," I said. "You are becoming quite the chef."

Cade put down his fork and looked at me with a serious expression. That was rare for him. "Scottie," he said (calling me by my first name was also rare), "I'm sorry I acted like such a heel this morning. Braddock and I— well—it's just better when we don't cross paths. I left the bakery worried that you wouldn't speak to me anymore, and frankly, that would make life unbearable. The truth is, in case you hadn't already figured this out, I really, really like you. And yes, those are the same words I used in third grade when I finally got the courage to talk to Sally McBurney, the cutest girl in class and yes, being a published author, I should have been able to come up with something much more profound and noteworthy and now, of course, I'm rambling like a fool who—"

I reached across and took his hand. "Stop. You had me at 'I really, really like you.' Because I feel the same way, Cade. I can't imagine not having you to talk to."

I released his hand and, in pleasantly awkward silence, we both picked up our forks. Something told me, if we hadn't had a dining table between us, there might have been a kiss.

Or maybe that was just wishful thinking on my part. Or was that really what I wished for? A kiss would take us around the corner on this relationship. It could complicate things. It could actually put us at a disadvantage when it came to being friends. If things didn't work out, could we stay friends? The odds were against us. It was a small town. We'd have to pass each other constantly and avoid eye contact. As much as I wanted that kiss (at least I thought I did), I was sure it would only complicate everything else about our wonderful friendship.

"Penny for your thoughts, Ramone?" Cade asked.

"Uh, oh, I was just thinking about how good your mac and cheese is."

Of course, he didn't buy my lame excuse. "Hmm, funny, I was thinking the same thing." There was a twinkle in his eye that assured me he was having the same mental debate about that darn, elusive and yet ever-present notion of a kiss.

seven

. . .

THE MORNING RUSH WAS OVER, and I paused for a cup of coffee for the first time since I left the house. Jack was working on something at the mixing bowl. "No coffee break?" I asked.

He picked up a cutting board full of walnuts and pushed the chopped nuts into the mixing bowl. "Not this morning. I had three cups before I left the house." He paused his task to look my direction. "So much caffeine I could have run here. I'm determined to show Miss—what's her name?"

His tone assured me he was talking about Crystal. "Miss Miramont."

"Yeah, that's it. I'm going to show her that she should never judge a baker by his gruff exterior." He turned on the mixer. The aroma of sugar and rum filled the air. He turned it off and brought me a spoonful to taste. "This is the filling."

"Hmm, delicious. I'd just eat that on a spoon. Forget the cake and frosting."

"I wonder if it needs a little more rum." He returned to the mixing bowl. The poor man had wound himself up about getting the cake just right.

I walked over and put my arm around his shoulders for a squeeze. (His shoulder span was so broad; I couldn't get a real squeeze in.) "Even though that woman has probably eaten at some of the most expensive restaurants in the world, I guarantee your Lady Baltimore will be the best cake she's ever tasted."

Jack looked unsure about that but he smiled. "Thanks, Scottie."

I returned to my cup of coffee and drank the last of it. The night before, I'd planned to get home by nine, but Cade and I had such a good time, talking and laughing and just hanging out, it was hard to pull myself away. My head didn't hit the pillow until way past ten, and the alarm woke me from a deep sleep. I poured myself another cup but put it down when the front door opened.

Jack turned off the mixer. I put up a hand to stop him. "I'll get it. You keep working on Lady Baltimore."

Rusty Simmer was standing at the counter, pacing excitedly as he perused the pastries behind the glass. He was moving quickly and energetically as if he, too, had drunk too much coffee. Seeing him in the semi-agitated state reminded me of how oddly he'd acted in Amy's shop.

"Morning, Rusty." I said it gently, but his face snapped up as if his name had come with a splash of cold water.

"Morning, Scottie. I didn't see you step out from the back." He rubbed his hands together a few times as he stared at the pastries. "So hungry I can't decide. I skipped dinner last night because—" He shook his head as if chiding himself not to say more.

"Everything all right?" I asked. "I'll have those cookies ready at closing today."

"Cookies?" he asked.

"For the club meeting," I reminded him.

"Oh, right, the club." He pulled out his phone and looked at it, then stuck it back in his pocket. Something was up with Rusty, and I was sure it had to do with the cigar box. "I think I'll have two cherry Danish."

I grabbed the tongs and a bag. "Where is Cameron this morning?"

Rusty sighed. "He's angry at me because he lost at chess yesterday afternoon. It always takes him a day to get over losing." It seemed Hannah had not exaggerated about the two men being competitive.

"That's a shame, Rusty. I'm sure he'll come around soon." He followed me over to the register.

He paused before pulling out his wallet and looked back to make sure we were alone. "Can I tell you something? I've got a big secret, and I'm just dying to tell someone."

"Of course, Rusty. I'm honored you chose me. I'm pretty good at keeping secrets." It was hard not to smile at how excited and anxious he was to tell someone.

"It'll be big news and out in the open soon enough… if it turns out the way I hope."

"My goodness, Rusty, you certainly have my curiosity piqued."

Rusty looked around again. He leaned to the side to glance back to the kitchen area. Jack was still running the mixer. He was satisfied that his secret wouldn't be heard and scrunched down slightly. "I think I've found a 1943 Lincoln copper penny." He sucked back as if what he'd said had just caused a minor explosion. I tried to mirror his excitement, but it was hard. Something told me I wasn't the best candidate to hear his big secret.

"That's amazing, Rusty. Excuse my ignorance—aren't all pennies copper and with Lincoln's profile?"

Rusty was shaking his head before I finished my question. "In 1943, the mint switched to making steel pennies because copper and nickel, the usual metals, were needed in the war effort. But they accidentally struck out thirty or forty of the pennies in copper before they were switched to steel."

I wasn't completely ignorant, apparently, because now his giddiness made sense. "So, there are only thirty or forty in the world with that date that are made of copper?"

Rusty's face split with a pleased smile. "Exactly. One sold recently for over a million dollars."

I straightened in surprise. "A million-dollar penny? I guess the next time I see one on the sidewalk, I'll make the effort to pick it up."

"That's right. You never know—it might be a rare coin. Unfortunately, there are a lot of fake 1943 copper pennies, so I'm waiting for a call from an expert. I've sent him photos and close-ups of the coin. I'm not entirely sure he can give me a definite answer from photos."

"By any chance—Rusty—does all this have to do with the cigar box you found in Henry's things?"

The question flustered him, and he got defensive. "I bought that box fair and square. Not my fault Henry and Amy never looked inside. Or maybe they did and just thought it was a regular old penny."

"Of course, like you said, Rusty. You bought the box fair and square. I've heard of people buying a painting from a thrift store only to find it's a rare, valuable piece of art. It happens. You haven't told Cameron about this yet?"

"I tried to call him yesterday to let him know, but he wouldn't answer. He was still sore about losing to me in chess. Then I decided I should find out for certain first. I'd never hear the end of Cam's teasing if I'd gotten worked up about a fake. That's why I'd appreciate it if you kept this between us," Rusty said. "No sense counting my chickens yet." He shivered with excitement. "But my intuition tells me I found a treasure."

"I hope so, Rusty. Maybe you'll have something big to announce at tonight's meeting."

Rusty couldn't stop smiling as he paid for his Danish and walked out.

Jack came out from the back with another spoonful of filling. "I put in a little more rum."

I tasted the spoonful. "Oh my, everyone at the shower is going to be tipsy."

Jack laughed. "Too much rum?"

"Little bit, yeah. I liked the previous spoonful. Perfect balance of all the flavors."

"Right. Then that's the ratio of ingredients I'll use." He glanced toward the window. "Was that Rusty? Did he have anything interesting to say? Has he found a gold doubloon?" Jack laughed. I'd been sworn to secrecy, so I couldn't tell him that he might have found something close.

"Just the usual chat. He did say that Cameron is not speaking to him at the moment because of a game of chess."

Jack shook his head. "Not the first time those two have been in a huff about that."

"I guess they're quite competitive." I wondered how Cameron would feel about his buddy finding an extremely rare coin. "I'm going to make the raspberry thumbprints for their cookie tray."

"Sounds good. And Lady Baltimore will have to wait. I've got some cupcakes to frost."

eight
...

WHILE JACK WAS on his lunchbreak, Esme texted that she'd bought a big sub sandwich and couldn't eat all of it. She insisted I eat the other half. Esme Adams was in her late thirties, and she owned the delightful bookstore, Nine Lives Bookshop, next door to the bakery. She'd helped me pick colors and décor for my bakery, and we became fast friends. I needed a good sit down with Esme. And the topic was going to be boys, or in this case, men.

Jack came back from his lunchbreak. He was sliding off his coat as he walked inside. "It's colder than I expected today. I'm sure ready for some warm temperatures. Oh, and I stopped in Roxi's to grab a sandwich for lunch. Rusty was in there holding a small court with Roxi and a few other women. He was telling them something about a rare penny. He said it could be worth a million dollars." Jack chuckled. "I don't see how that's possible unless it truly is a lucky penny that grants wishes. I've carried a few of those around in my pockets, but wishes were never granted."

Apparently, the top-secret coin find wasn't so top secret, after all. I wondered if Rusty had gotten confirmation from the expert. For something so rare, it didn't seem a photo authentication would be enough.

"He mentioned something to me about a rare copper penny, but he told me not to tell anyone about it." I laughed. "Going next door to the bookshop."

Esme was helping none other than Rusty Simmer when I stepped inside. A few people were sitting in the various seating areas reading and sipping the complimentary tea Esme provided on a tea cart. Earl, Esme's huge gray tabby, sashayed over to see me. I stopped to rub his head.

"I think there are a few books about rare coins in this aisle," Esme said. She winked at me. "Lunch is in my office."

I wandered past the bookshelves and display tables and headed down the short hallway to Esme's office. It was a cramped space much like my office, but she had it so well organized there was room for a desk and a small bistro table and chairs. Three boxes of new books sat in one corner. She had not oversold the massive sandwich. Even cut in half, it was big.

Esme came into the office. She had her short black hair pushed back by a paisley hairband, and she was wearing a sweater with a bookworm embroidered on the front. "It's so cute," Esme said with a quiet voice. "Rusty thinks he's found a valuable penny. I don't know much about coins, but he insists it could be worth a million dollars."

I smiled and shook my head. "That secret is spreading faster than a wildfire in a parched forest."

Esme sat down at the table. "What do you mean?"

"Rusty came into the bakery this morning looking giddy and anxious. He finally confessed to me that he had a big secret, and he was bursting to tell someone. Of course, I told him I'd keep my lips sealed. But, apparently, my skills at secret keeper weren't needed because he's been telling everyone."

"Guess he really was bursting." She unfolded a napkin for her lap. "Now, I'm not a coin expert and few people are, but I thought that sounded a little crazy. How could a penny be worth that much money?"

"Rusty explained that it had something to do with a mistake at the mint. They were supposed to be producing steel pennies because they needed copper for the war. Thirty or forty copper ones were made before they caught the mistake."

"Ah, so the value is in the rareness." Esme took half the sandwich and handed me the other half. It weighed a good pound. "Is that a sandwich or what?" she asked. "It's from Pike's Sandwich shop near the resort. I had to drive up there to pick up a rare copy of *Little Women*. I had an online customer ask me if I knew where to pick one up, and I happened to know a collector who had one for sale. But that's not the interesting part of my morning," she said but then stopped. "Or maybe I shouldn't."

I lifted a brow. "Really? You don't actually think I'm going to let you leave that cliffhanger in the air with no satisfying conclusion?"

"I guess that wouldn't be very friend-like."

"Well, you are sharing your gigantic sandwich with me, but I'd still like to hear about the interesting part of your morning."

"Fine, if you're going to be so insistent," she said with a laugh. "Marla, the woman with the rare book, owns a fine jewelry shop about a mile from the resort, lots of sparkly diamonds and platinum and rich woman's bling. And so, who walks in, of course, but the ultimate rich woman, Crystal Miramont. Do you think she'll change her name after they're married? I mean the Miramont name seems like a big deal up here."

"It is and I hadn't really given it a thought." I hadn't meant to sound pouty about it, but it came out that way.

Esme pressed fingers to her lips. "I'm sorry. I guess Crystal Miramont is not a good topic for lunch conversation." I'd told Esme about my silly crush on Dalton. She'd been my sounding board about my unusual friendship with Cade, and anecdotes about Dalton were always peppered into the chat whenever I brought it up. Somehow, the two men had become intertwined like one tangled strand.

"That's all right. Tell the story, please."

"If you're sure." Esme took a nibble of her sandwich and sip of her water. "Apparently, Crystal decided the diamond stud earrings she owned weren't good enough for her wedding day. She complained they were too small, and she didn't like the cut of the diamonds. So, Marla pulled out a velvet tray of diamond studs for Crystal to peruse while Marla went to the back to get the book. Crystal has been in my bookshop a few times, but she glanced my direction and smiled the way someone might smile at a stranger. I guess she didn't recognize me."

I rolled my eyes and continued eating.

"I know, she doesn't bother getting to know us little folk," Esme added. "Then something funny and kind of odd happened—" Someone rang the bell on the front desk. Esme put down her sandwich. "To be continued. That's probably Rusty." Esme hurried out to help Rusty. I pulled my phone out to check a text that had come through while Esme was telling her story. It was from Jack.

"We're out of pecans. Wanna stop by Roxi's on your way back to pick up a bag?"

"Sure thing," I texted back.

Esme returned. "He found the book he wanted. That poor guy is going to be disappointed if it turns out he just has a run-of-the-mill, old penny." Esme sat down. "Now, where was I?"

"You were at the funny, odd part," I reminded her.

"That's right. So, I'm standing at the counter waiting for Marla. Wasn't much else for me to do since I didn't have a cool ten thousand in my checking account for a diamond tennis bracelet."

"You would never, ever wear a diamond tennis bracelet."

Esme shrugged. "You're right. It's the last thing I'd buy with that ten grand I don't have. Crystal was very busy with the studs. She even had one of those small loupes, I think they're called, the special magnifying glass a jeweler uses to check the quality or authenticity of a jewel."

I laughed. "Guess she's expecting people to walk up to her on the wedding day and inspect her diamond studs for flaws."

"I thought it was pretentious but then, 'pretentious' is her middle name. Anyhow, there she was, leaning over the diamonds, checking each one for clarity, when Dalton stepped up to the front window of the store. He was looking at the display in the window. He spotted me first and waved. It seemed that he was about to come inside. That was when he noticed the other customer at the counter. He saw Crystal, but she didn't see him. Instead of coming inside, he took a quick turn and walked away." Esme sat back and took a breath. "Weird, right?"

My thirteen-year-old self was telling me—he didn't want to see her because he doesn't like her anymore. But my forty-something self, which was not nearly as fun, told me he didn't want her to see him because he was probably there to buy her a gift. Seeing him would ruin the surprise. I said as much to Esme, and she was disappointed in that explanation.

We tackled our massive sandwich halves as best we could. I'd come over to talk about Cade and the maybe, possible, tentative kiss, but after the Crystal story, I preferred to talk about other things. The customers had other ideas. The bell rang when Esme was midbite.

"You need to find an assistant," I told her as she stood up.

"I know. Maybe we could clone Jack," she said as she hurried away.

nine

. . .

"BUTTERFLIES, BE STILL," I muttered to myself as I crossed the street to the market. Dalton's ranger truck was parked out front, so it was easy to assume he was inside picking up lunch or a snack. We ran nearly smack-dab into each other as he walked out and I attempted to walk in. He was holding one of Roxi's homemade sandwiches.

His cocoa brown eyes sparkled. "Scottie, almost ran you down. If you're looking for ham and cheese, I just bought the last one. But I'm not averse to sharing, thanks to our second grade teacher, Miss"—his finely chiseled jaw shifted back and forth in thought—"her name had something to do with the *Peanuts* comic strip," he continued.

I snapped my fingers. "That's right. Miss Linus. That's the year I started school in Ripple Creek, and she let me hold the class teddy bear all day to help me feel at home. A new kid couldn't have asked for a better teacher."

"Especially after what you'd been through." Dalton's expression turned thoughtful. "I remember my mom telling me that little Scottie Ramone, the new girl, had lost both her parents in a tragic accident. At that age, it was impossible to believe that something like that could happen, that someone could lose both their parents. But you powered through. You were always kind and funny. I doubt many kids could have gone through those years so stoically."

I felt my cheeks warm but couldn't stop the blush. "That's nice of you to say, Dalton. Don't forget, I had the world's most amazing grandmother to fill the void."

"That you did and still do." We stood in silence for a second. His gaze felt nice, comforting.

"It was good seeing you, Scottie."

"You too." He walked back to his truck and smiled at me before getting inside.

I thought about Esme's story. I hoped Dalton wasn't making a mistake going through with the marriage if he was unhappy. I'd almost made the same mistake. Big weddings sometimes made it seem the decision was irreversible, as if once the caterer and florists had been given a down payment, there was no turning back. I knew firsthand, cancelling a wedding was expensive and stressful and earned the canceller a lot of threats and hateful phone calls, but it was a small price to pay to not end up in a future where happiness was out of reach.

Roxi was sweeping up a spilled bag of rice as I walked inside. She stopped moving the broom when she looked up. "Jack said you needed pecans. I put them up at the counter.

I'll be there in a second. I had a bag of rice go rogue on me as I was placing it on the shelf."

"I see that. I had the same thing happen with bread flour a few weeks ago. Big mess." The produce aisle was rich with the fragrance of fresh strawberries. I decided to buy some for Nana. She loved to put them on her oatmeal.

Amy Dency, the owner of the antique shop, walked in as I was picking out the plumpest berries. Roxi looked up again from the mess on the floor. "Hey, Amy, we've still got a chicken sandwich in the fridge. I know those are your favorite."

"Thanks, Roxi." Amy looked slightly glum about something. Even her tone was glum.

I finished picking the berries and carried them up to the counter. Roxi picked up the last runaway grains of rice and met me at the register. She pulled out the bag of pecans. Amy reached the counter with her chicken sandwich and a bottle of tea.

Roxi smiled at Amy, seemingly not noticing that she looked distraught. "No barbecue chips today?"

"No, my doctor told me to cut down on salt," Amy said.

Regina hurried into the market. Whenever she was doing her race-walk, it meant she had some gossip or something intriguing to report. Regina Sharpe owned the gift shop next to the market. She was one of Nana's dear friends, and while my grandmother liked a bit of gossip now and then, she complained that Regina positively lived and breathed the stuff. She obviously had something good to tell because she was biting her lip in excitement.

"Have you all heard about the million-dollar penny?" It seemed the secret continued to be anything but secret.

Amy placed her food items on the counter with a plunk. "If you're talking about Rusty's rare coin find, then you haven't heard the whole story."

Regina looked disappointed that she didn't have the whole story. She decided to defend her position as top gossip in town. "I'm sure I have. Rusty Simmer, as some of us well know, collects rare coins for a hobby. He was searching through some old stuff, and he found what he thought looked like a rare penny. Something about steel or copper." Regina waved off what she considered unimportant details from a noteworthy story. "He sent photos of the coin to an expert, and the expert thought he had a rare penny. One that might be worth as much as a million dollars. Can you imagine that?"

"Rusty was in here just this morning telling me about the valuable penny," Roxi said. Regina slumped slightly. She was coming to the conclusion that she was not the only person in town privy to the rare coin story. "At that time, Rusty was still waiting for confirmation from an expert that it was real. Seems as though he's heard good news since then. Although, even he admitted that it's hard to get rock-solid verification from photos. Rusty seemed confident that he had the real thing."

Amy scoffed. "If it's true, he'll be sharing those million dollars with yours truly." That comment grabbed everyone's attention. I knew why she said it, but Roxi and Regina looked perplexed.

"Why, Amy, I didn't realize you and Rusty Simmer were—" Regina paused to search for the right word. "Well, I didn't know you two were an item." She slumped again in disappointment because she was sure that was a piece of gossip she'd missed out on.

Amy laughed harshly. "Rusty is old enough to be my father. Of course, we're not an item." (In Amy's defense—it was a rather silly assumption.) "The old stuff Rusty was looking through"—she looked pointedly at Regina—"were antiques in my shop. He found an old cigar box. I'm convinced he opened it and discovered the coin. He very stealthily bought the box without letting me know there was something of value inside. It was basically stealing. Scottie knows. She was there."

Roxi and Regina turned my direction. I was hoping to remain on the sidelines of this conversation, but now I'd been pulled into the center of it. And I probably knew more than Amy about the cigar box. I wasn't about to start any more trouble with what I knew.

"Uh, I did see Rusty looking through the old stuff that Henry Voight brought in. I think I saw him with a cigar box."

"Then maybe the coin belongs to Henry," Roxi suggested and rightfully so.

Amy's arms crossed defensively. "I paid Henry good money for those antiques and that cigar box. I own all of it."

"But you called it stealing when Rusty took the box without telling you about the coin. Aren't you doing the same thing by not telling Henry about the coin?" Regina asked it confidently, then instantly shrank back when confronted with Amy's withering scowl.

"Henry should have looked through the cigar box before he sold it to me," Amy said. It was a weak defense considering what she'd just said about Rusty stealing from her.

Roxi and Regina were thinking the same thing, but neither pointed out the hypocrisy. I didn't either. I wasn't invested enough in the whole debacle to stick my neck out on the topic. And so far, this whole thing was based on a somewhat questionable authentication process. Maybe the coin was worthless, and everyone was getting in a lather about nothing.

I gave Roxi the money for the pecans and said quick goodbyes. I didn't have time to stand around and debate the rights and wrongs of it. I had a cookie tray to finish.

ten
. . .

JACK HAD BEEN OPENING the bakery most mornings. He was, as he put it, a perpetual early riser. I handled closing up. He'd already wiped down the work counters and mopped the floor. All I had to do was clean the glass on the display cabinets. I was in the middle of that task when there was a knock on the bakery door. It was Cade. No cardboard signage this time. No butterflies either but I was happy to see him. It was possible I was putting far too much stock in those fickle butterflies.

I walked to the door and unlocked it. Cade stepped inside. "Cold again." He was wearing a winter coat and gloves. "I keep waking up to a brilliant blue sky, and I think, oh, it's nice outside. Spring is here. Then I step out the door and reality hits. No spring, just a glacial chill under a pretty sky. Anyhow, I'm out walking because I've been sitting at the computer all morning, and my heart was thumping on my chest saying, 'Hello there, did you forget about me?' One of the hazards of being an author."

"Well, I've been on my feet all day, but if you stopped by to find a walking partner, I wouldn't mind a brisk walk to the park and back. Being on one's feet and exercising are very different."

"Great. Do you need me to do anything? Although no mopping of floors. I hate that job. My mom used to leave a list of chores on the refrigerator for me when I got home from school, and mopping the kitchen floor was always top of the list."

"Well, you're in luck. We won't have to rekindle any of that childhood trauma because the floor has already been mopped. In fact, I'm done. I just need to get my coat and gloves."

Minutes later, Cade and I were strolling toward the park. He was right. The gorgeous sky certainly held the promise of spring, but I knew too well that a blue sky meant nothing at this altitude.

"I'd say another month of this cold and then we'll wake up one morning and think—time to pull out the shorts and sandals," I said. "I remember one particularly brutal spring when I was a teenager. It was still snowing in June. We were on summer break and still wearing our gloves and beanies. I told Nana it was time to move south or west. I told her I couldn't spend one more day layered in sweaters and coats. Two months later I was complaining that it was far too hot in the cottage."

There was a lot of activity in the park considering it was a chilly day. A few children were riding bicycles around the path, but most of the action was at the chess tables. I spotted Cameron standing with a few regulars. He'd picked up the cookie tray on the way to chess. Surprisingly, Henry was with them. He didn't usually play chess. Rusty wasn't in the bunch. Maybe he was home guarding his valuable coin, I thought wryly.

"You thought you moved to a dull small town, but we have quite an exciting story happening right now," I said.

"You forget that a man was murdered on my property before any dust had settled on my furniture. And then there were the photography club murders, and I seem to remember a rather grisly Christmas murder of a gingerbread man. This town might be small, but dull? Never."

I nodded. "I suppose we have had our share of explosive events, but this one is the opposite of murder. Remember Rusty and his clandestine movements in the antique store?"

"Yes. He acted as if he was sneaking off with the secrets to the universe in that old cigar box."

We slowed our pace so I could tell him the story before we reached the chess table area. "Apparently, there was a rare coin in that box, one that might be worth a million dollars."

"I'd say the important word there is *might*. I've known a few people who got duped into paying big money for counterfeit art. Lots of fakes out there."

"That's the first thing I thought when Rusty told me his big secret. I was honored that he chose to tell me about the coin, only it turned out he was telling pretty much everyone in town. But that's not important. Rusty's somewhat of an expert himself, and he was convinced he'd found the real thing. He certainly had a profound reaction when he saw it in the box at the antique store. He sent some photos to an expert who said it looked genuine."

We reached the chess area. Henry was wearing the same 'I've been wronged' expression that Amy was wearing in the market. I was certain the conversation they were holding was about the coin.

"The tray is perfect," Cameron said. "Thank you for doing that on such short notice. We have a big meeting tonight. I expect all members to attend. A special guest, Daniel Lomax, a coin expert and appraiser, is coming."

"Does that have to do with Rusty's penny?" I asked.

"You mean *my penny*," Henry said sharply. Everything about his expression and tone reminded me of Amy. Henry was even crossing his arms defensively. "That penny belongs to me. It doesn't matter what Rusty says."

Ronald, one of the chess regulars, chuckled. "I was just telling Henry that Amy Dency said the exact same thing to her friend in the coffee shop."

"I purchased an old trunk once at an antique shop," Cade said. "It turned out to have some old magazines and newspapers inside. A few were worth a small amount of money. I certainly didn't feel I needed to take the items back to the antique shop."

"He's got a point," Ronald said. "I once found an old dollar bill inside a book I bought at a yard sale. I didn't rush back to the owners to hand over the money. It was in the book, and I bought the book."

"We're talking about a penny that might be worth a million dollars." Henry lowered his arms and straightened his posture. "That's not the same as a dollar bill or some old magazines."

"But shouldn't the same rules apply?" Ronald asked.

Henry shook his head adamantly. "I'm sure those rules don't apply to items of such value."

"Didn't you sell those things to Amy?" Dick asked. "Technically, Amy owned that cigar box when Rusty bought it."

Henry's face reddened with frustration. It seemed he'd come to the park to commiserate and lure people to his side, but that wasn't happening. "I had no idea that rare coin was in the box." He chuckled dryly and recrossed his arms. "If I had, I certainly wouldn't have sold it for the small amount Amy paid me."

"If you had opened the box, would you have known that the penny was rare?" Cameron asked. "Very few people would have recognized that penny as being rare and valuable. That's how heirlooms and valuable art pieces end up in thrift stores and flea markets."

Henry opened his mouth to protest, but Cameron put up a hand to stop him.

"Henry, before you get worked up about this penny, let's see what Mr. Lomax has to say. So far, Rusty has been relying on certification through photos. That is hardly considered the gold standard when it comes to verifying authenticity. It's entirely possible that Rusty has merely found one of the many well-made fakes floating around the collector's world. Rusty sure has gotten everyone in town up in arms about a penny that might only be worth one cent."

"Well, I'm not a member of your club, but you're sure going to see me tonight," Henry said. "If that penny is the real thing, then I want to know about it."

Cameron sighed loudly. "Amy has told me the same thing. But I'm sorry. Only dues-paying members are allowed to participate in discussions and partake of the treats." Cameron smiled at me. "It's a private club meeting."

Henry frowned in disappointment. "Well, either way, I'll want to know whether it's real or not."

Cade and I said goodbye and continued along the path. The lake in the middle of the park had only partially thawed. A pair of mallard ducks were resting on a floating piece of ice. A few patches of green were starting to show through the otherwise brown lawn on either side of the path.

"And you dared to call the town dull," Cade quipped.

"I misspoke. Silly might have been a better word. Whose side do you fall on in this debate?"

"Seems to me the box and the contents belong to Rusty. He bought the box."

I nodded. "That's what I think. But a million dollars is a big piece of pie. Maybe they can find a way to share the money."

Cade's laugh sent the ducks into the water.

"Don't be so cynical." I knuckled his arm.

"Not being cynical. I'm being pragmatic, and that is based

on everything I've witnessed in my forty-something years as a member of the human race. I just hope it doesn't get ugly."

"Like Cameron said—it might be a worthless fake. For Rusty's sake, I hope he's wrong, but for the town's sanity, I hope he's right."

eleven

. . .

THE BRISK WALK WAS INVIGORATING, but once I got in my car to drive home, I released a long, exhausted sigh. I'd stayed up too late the night before. I had firm plans of getting to bed much earlier tonight, but as Cade walked me to my car, he asked me out to dinner. A new Italian restaurant had opened near the resort and was receiving high praise. Cade had managed to snatch a reservation for dinner. How could I turn that down? The reservation was for seven o'clock. I told him I'd go as long as we could be back in Ripple Creek by nine.

    I drove home dreaming of a long, hot shower and a short nap before having to get ready for the dinner date. And that was what I was calling it—a date. Our relationship had no concise definition yet, but he'd made a reservation and invited me to dinner, so it was more than a "hey, Ramone, come eat mac and cheese" evening. I was sorting through the virtual closet in my head, trying to decided what to wear, when I turned the corner to Nana's house. Dalton's truck was parked out front. The butterflies fluttered their wings for a second, then settled back down. He was here to see Nana. She had a habit of inviting Dalton for soup and chili and pancakes. He never turned her down. I could see both of them sitting at the kitchen table, deep in a serious conversation.

I pulled into the driveway and considered waiting a few minutes. I didn't want to interrupt their chat, but Dalton glanced out the window and spotted me. I had no choice but to go inside.

"Scottie, we're here in the kitchen. Dalton is having some homemade chicken soup. Do you want a bowl?"

I wanted to save room for the Italian dinner, but turning down the soup would hurt her feelings. Besides that, the walk and long day at work had left me quite hungry. I was sure I could eat some soup and still have room for a plate of spaghetti.

"Sure, Nana, but just a cup," I called. "I'll be right there." I went to my room and changed out of my work clothes. I pulled on jeans and a sweater, combed my fingers through my hair and checked the mirror for facial flour streaks.

Dalton was hunched over his bowl of soup. He didn't see me at first. Something about his posture and the way he cradled the bowl of soup made him look like a lost little boy Nana had just rescued from a bad storm. Nana looked a little pensive as well. It seemed I hadn't misread what I saw through the kitchen window.

Nana put a cup of soup on the table. "Why only a cup? Too much taste testing at the bakery?" Her tone lightened. Now that I was there, the previous conversation, whatever it was about, was over.

"I'm going out to dinner," I said.

Dalton looked up at me. I didn't feel the need to elaborate. I didn't need to. He knew. He returned to his bowl of soup.

"Evie, I think this might be your best soup yet," Dalton said.

"Would you like another bowl?" she asked eagerly.

"No, I'm having dinner with Crystal later. I need to save room."

"Anything new happening in town?" I asked. I'd directed the question toward the local ranger, but Nana hopped in to answer it.

"Everyone is talking about Rusty Simmer finding a rare coin." She sat down to her bowl of soup.

Her comment made me laugh.

Nana looked at me. "What's so funny, Button? Did it turn out to be a fake? Oh, poor Rusty, he'll be devastated."

"No, it's not that. Rusty came in this morning, fidgety and nervous. He told me he was holding onto a big secret, and he was bursting to tell someone. He told me about his rare penny and swore me to secrecy and then went right out and told literally everyone he met. It's funny and cute. And I can tell you that the penny, whether genuine or not, has stirred up all kinds of controversy."

"I heard something about a million-dollar penny. I figured it was just one of those town rumors being blown out of proportion." Dalton's phone beeped. "Excuse me." He took the phone out to the front room to answer the call.

Nana was giving me a shifty-eyed look. It was her clumsy way of trying to tell me something was up with Dalton. Her smile returned the second he reached the kitchen.

"Evie, the soup was delicious. There's been an accident, nothing bad, but two cars are blocking the highway. I need to get out there." He picked up his bowl and like that little lost kid I saw earlier, he lifted the bowl and sipped it dry. He finished with a satisfied grin. "My mom used to get so mad when I did that as a kid."

Nana laughed. "It's the best way to finish a bowl of soup."

He smiled at my grandmother. "I really needed this, Evie. Thanks." His eyes barely flicked my direction before he placed the bowl in the sink and walked out.

Nana waited until the truck started up and pulled away. "That poor boy is so lost."

I smiled into my cup. I hadn't misread that either. "He looked sad when I saw you two through the kitchen window." Before Nana could continue, I reminded myself to take everything she said with the proverbial grain of salt. Nana was biased in her opinions about Dalton's marriage to Crystal. She'd somehow convinced herself that they weren't suited for each other and that we would end up together, putting a nice and neat fairytale ending on my decades-long crush.

"Dalton texted that he needed someone to talk to," Nana said. "I told him I'd made chicken soup. He rushed right over.

It was sweet really. Poor guy was in desperate need of a sympathetic ear."

"Why was he upset? I ran into him earlier at Roxi's, and he seemed to be in good spirits. We talked about our second-grade teacher, Miss Linus."

Nana's face smoothed with a fond memory. "Miss Linus was a wonderful teacher."

"I agree. But back to Dalton. What's going on that he badly needed to borrow my personal sympathetic ear? Not that I mind sharing my good fortune with others." I reached over and squeezed her hand.

"Thank you, Button. I guess all my years on this planet have given me a few wise nuggets of advice to share, but I didn't know how to help him with this. He needs to solve this problem on his own."

"Problem?" I asked. If I was smart, I'd have ended the conversation and not kept prodding. But I badly wanted to know what had Dalton upset.

"It's just those notorious pre-wedding jitters." Nana stood and picked up our dishes. "Dalton is having second thoughts about marrying Crystal. I reminded him that it was totally normal this close to a wedding." She sat back down. "I used you as an example."

"You did? Nana, I don't know if my situation was the best example. My jitters weren't just jitters. I had a major bout of trepidation just hours before my rehearsal dinner."

Nana smiled coyly down at her hands.

"You used that example on purpose." I was surprised it took me so long to see through her scheme.

Nana shrugged. "I thought it was an appropriate example. I used the word jitters a few seconds ago, but your word *trepidation* is far more accurate. Dalton is having some serious doubts about the whole thing."

I sat back, slightly stunned. "You didn't tell him to break things off, did you?" Suddenly I wondered just how far my grandmother would go to secure my happy ending. But that ending was long gone. It was a teenage romance ending, and we were far past that time in our lives.

"Of course not, Button. I'd never do that. I assured him it was jitters more than once. I also told him he needed to really take time to reflect on this marriage because there was still time to change his mind. I told him if you're not both going to be wildly happy as a married couple, then he should think twice about it."

"You've never made the commitment, Nana. You're the wisest person I know and your advice is always profound and spot on, but I think you might have stepped out of your area of expertise on this one. I doubt many couples are wildly happy. It's hard living with another person, someone with different habits and likes than your own. Happiness for a good portion of the time—that's the goal most married couples aspire to. 'Wildly happy' is only at the beginning of a relationship when love and passion are still fresh."

My words caused her to frown. "Oh Button, I don't think that's true. And I don't think wildly happy is too lofty of a goal. Now, you said you were going out to dinner." The lines around her eyes crinkled. "With handsome Cade?"

"Yes, with handsome Cade. He's taking me to the new

Italian restaurant up by the resort. And now, since I still smell like frosting and cinnamon—"

"You say that like it's a bad thing," Nana teased.

I laughed. "Could be worse, I suppose. Still, I think a long, hot shower is in order." I stood up and leaned over to kiss her on the cheek. "I'm glad Dalton has found someone to talk to. Just make sure you keep your advice from an impartial perspective and not a matchmaker one."

twelve

. . .

I'D DECIDED to wear one of my nicer dresses, navy blue with a low neckline, a hem that showed just enough leg and a flirty bounce to the skirt. I pulled two strands of hair back and clipped them behind my head with a barrette. Nana whistled as I stepped into the front room.

"It's been a long time since I've seen you dressed up like that, Button." Her eyes grew glossy. "You look so much like your mom." My memories of my parents were so sparse, scattered and unclear that I had to rely almost solely on photos to remember them. I did remember thinking that my mom was the prettiest mom in the world.

"Do I? I hope so, Nana." I switched some of my essentials; wallet, phone, lipstick from my usual daily sack (at least that was what I called it) to a blue clutch. "I'm feeling a little nervous. I know it's just Cade, but most of the time we only hang out in a casual way, a glass of wine in his kitchen or a walk to the park. We've never really sat down to a nice dinner at a restaurant."

"So, this is a date?" she asked. "He's finally made a move *that* direction?"

"I consider this a date because it has all the elements of a date, but I have no idea if it's a move *that* direction or not. To be honest, Nana, having someone like *that* right now seems like more than I can handle. The bakery takes up most of my waking hours. I had to rest for an hour just to catch a second wind for the dinner."

"That's understandable, but you need things outside of the bakery for a full life."

"I know."

There was a knock on the door. "Is my lipstick all right?" I asked Nana.

She laughed. "It's perfect. I guess it has been a while since you've been on a proper date. Shall I invite him in and grill him about where he's taking you and what his intentions are?" she quipped.

I rolled my eyes and walked to the door. Cade had pulled on a suit and tie. He looked stunning. He seemed pleased with my attire as well. His whistle was a little lower and more suggestive than Nana's.

"Wow, Ramone, you clean up nice."

"I can say the same about you. Never took you for a suit and tie man."

Cade looked down at his coat and brushed away a few invisible particles. "This old thing? Found it in the back of my closet."

I lifted a brow. "That is not a back of the closet suit."

"You're right. It's my one small investment to look like a presentable person for funerals, weddings and dates with hot women in blue dresses."

"I'll just get my coat."

Cade stepped inside. Nana whistled again. (There seemed to be a lot of that going around.) "Look at you in a suit. You two look like you should have paparazzi following you around with cameras."

Cade laughed. "I couldn't agree more." He helped me on with my coat, and we said goodbye to Nana and walked out the door.

The road up to the resort was quiet. There was still snow on the slopes, but peak ski season was over. A half-moon sat high in the sky. It helped illuminate some of the thick landscape bordering the curvy highway.

I caught Cade smiling down at my legs more than once. "Seriously, Ramone, you look great."

"You have seen my legs before. I wear shorts all summer," I reminded him.

"Yet, somehow, that's not the same as seeing them peer out from under a dress."

"Well, you and that suit make quite a splash too."

"Then I'm glad I decided to pull it out of the dry-cleaning bag."

"Funerals and weddings, eh?"

Cade laughed. "A few."

"And only girls in blue dresses?" I asked.

"Yes, so it's a good thing you chose that one tonight, otherwise the whole thing would have been called off. Any more news on the ever-important coin discovery?" He reached to turn down the defroster.

"Haven't heard anything noteworthy, but I suppose all of it will come to a head tonight at one of the most-anticipated coin collectors club meetings in years. That last part was based on my own observation. I have no idea if it's truly the most-anticipated or not. Cameron is bringing in the expert to give a thumbs up or down on the penny. Thumbs up means it's worth some serious bucks, and thumbs down means it's worth a cent or less, I suppose, if it's fake."

"That's a pretty big value spread," Cade said. "I'm interested to see what happens."

We pulled into the parking lot. "I think I can already smell the garlic," I said. The outside of the restaurant was modern with a lot of angles and corners. I pulled my coat closer around me. The dress might have looked pretty, but it wasn't very practical for the cold spring weather. My legs were freezing by the time we stepped inside. Fortunately, two large hearths, one on each side of the restaurant, had blazing fires. Gray and blue flooring was dotted with round tables covered in satiny white tablecloths, and the chairs were upholstered with copper and teal velvet. Blown glass pendants hung over each table, providing just enough light to see your plate. Soft music played through the room, and servers were dressed in tuxedos. The aromas floating around held the promise of a delicious meal.

Cade let the hostess know we had reservations, and we followed her to a table near the back of the restaurant. I was focused on the décor and imported tile floor and didn't notice who was sitting at the next table until Cade pulled out my chair to sit. My gaze crashed right into Dalton's as I sat down, destroying any attempt at a ladylike descent to the plush chair. My bottom landed with a thud. Cade was also now aware of our dining neighbors. Only Crystal hadn't noticed. She was busy running her expensively manicured fingers over the screen on her phone.

"Penelope is still looking for the right gloves to go with the bridesmaid gown. I've sent her at least half a dozen links." She dropped the phone in her clutch and, for the first time, looked up. Her mouth twisted into a sour lemon pout. She did, however, manage to flash a vibrant smile toward my date. I'd been looking forward to the evening, but now I wished, more than ever, that I was tucked in my cozy bed. I sensed some tension coming from my dinner partner as well.

Crystal was the first to speak up, unfortunately. "Do you two come here often? It's fabulous, isn't it? I hope it wasn't too hard getting reservations. My family has a standing reservation. All we have to do is call and they have a table waiting."

"Funny, all I had to do was call too," Cade said.

I lifted my hand to hide a grin. Dalton, on the other hand, looked as if he wanted nothing more than to slip under the table and disappear.

"It's Mr. Rafferty, right?" Crystal asked with a bat of her fake eyelashes. (At least I hoped they were fake. Extensions, at the very least.)

"Yes, Cade is fine."

"A few of my friends are big fans. I haven't read your books. I'm afraid I'm more into romance novels. They were very excited when I told them you lived in the area."

Cade nodded. "Very kind of you to say."

"Scottie, I hardly recognized you in that dress," Crystal said. "That color and style suits you." She sat back to make sure I noticed she was wearing one of her skin tight, designer dresses.

"That dress suits you too," I said. It would suit someone a size smaller better, I wanted to say but kept that part to myself.

"Cade," she said with newfound familiarity, "you must order the Rothschild Merlot to go with your meal. It's a little pricey but so worth it."

Dalton's jaw was clenched, but this time it had nothing to do with Cade. He leaned over. "Why don't we let them get on with their date," he said harshly to Crystal, then he looked at our table. "Enjoy your meal."

Crystal looked more than a little put out by his request. She wriggled on the velvet chair and picked up her menu. Cade tapped my foot with his. I picked up my menu, too, mostly to hide my amused grin. It was going to be an awkward evening, but I was wearing a dress and Cade was wearing a suit, and I was resolved to make the most of it.

thirteen

. . .

THE FOOD and company were great. The dinner date would have been perfect if not for our table neighbors. Cade and I tried hard to ignore them, and it seemed Dalton was trying his best, too. But Crystal talked loudly as if she was sitting at happy hour with a group of friends in the middle of a raucous sports bar. Her topics ranged from the original one about the bridesmaid's gloves to her dilemma on where to place the wedding cake during the reception. "After all," she'd said extra loudly, "a ten-thousand-dollar wedding cake needs to be the center of attention." Dalton looked embarrassed about her behavior.

Cade had a good loud laugh about all of it as we left the restaurant. As promised, he had me home by nine. The whole scene at the restaurant had been so comical and, frankly, stressful, any chance of a romantic kiss at the end had been obliterated.

I was out the second my head hit the pillow, but the alarm still pulled me from a deep sleep. I was a good thirty minutes late. Jack already had breads in the ovens when I arrived. For the next few hours, we swept around and past each other with trays of cookies and pastries. We managed to have everything on display and frosted and cut by opening. I switched to a clean apron as I glanced at the front of the shop. Everything looked delicious and ready to go.

Jack carried out the last batch of bread.

"We, my friend, are a well-oiled machine," I said.

Jack paused to take in our morning's accomplishments. "You're right about that." The door opened, and Jack smiled and winked at me. I turned around. Dalton always looked splendid in uniform. This morning, the uniform looked more crumpled than usual. In fact, Dalton looked more crumpled, as if he was wearing the weight of the world on his shoulders.

"That looks like a cherry-Danish-followed-by-a-brownie-chaser-at-lunch sort of face if I've ever seen one," I said.

He put up a hand before I could slide open the cabinet door. "No, I've got to cut down. Way too many treats lately. I think I've been trying to make myself happy with sweets."

"Uh, I believe that is what we women do when we're unhappy. Men go out and offroad their trucks on a muddy trail. And that ends my stereotyping speech for the morning." My attempt to put a smile on his face didn't work. I moved to stand directly across from him. I could see literal worry lines all over his handsome face. "Anything I can do to help?" I asked. He knew I wasn't talking about pastries.

Dalton took a deep breath. "Actually, I came in here to apologize for the way Crystal acted last night. She's just so wound up about this wedding. I hope she didn't ruin your night."

"Nope, Cade and I had a great time. That restaurant is good. I'm not sure if it's as fabulous as all the hype would have us believe, but it's a nice place for a dinner date."

His eyes lifted. "So, it *was* a date. I thought you two were just friends."

I stared back at him without saying a word.

He nodded. "Right, none of my business. Well, I'm glad she didn't ruin your evening."

"Not at all. And, like you said, I'm sure she's just a little energized because of the wedding."

His mouth tilted. "'Energized' is a nice way to put it." He gazed at me over the top of the display cases. I was expecting him to say goodbye. Instead, he moved closer. "When did you realize you needed to stop the wedding with Jonathan? Was it the just the occasional feelings of doubt or because he did things to annoy you? Was it one thing that really nailed your decision?"

I wasn't expecting this turn in conversation. I had to remind myself that, like Nana, I was coming from a biased view of the whole thing. "It wasn't one thing. It was an entire list of things, but mostly, I came to the heartbreaking conclusion that I didn't love him as much as I thought. Jonathan and I wanted different things, different futures, and he was expecting me to give up my own dreams and follow his path."

Dalton nodded. "That all makes sense." He forced a weak smile. "I'm glad I stopped in."

"Sure I can't interest you in a Danish?"

"Maybe just one."

He was taking out his wallet as I put the pastry in the bag. "No charge this morning." I smiled as I handed it to him. "It's on the house."

Our fingers touched as he took the bag. "Thanks, Scottie."

As he walked out, Cameron Burke stepped in with a man who looked to be about fifty. He was a snappy dresser with an expensive looking sweater, nice slacks and shiny leather loafers. The gold watch on his wrist glittered under the lights. His hair was slicked back with some kind of greasy product, and his aftershave nearly drowned out the bakery smells.

"Morning, Cameron." I smiled politely at his friend.

"Morning, Scottie. This is Daniel Lomax, a friend of mine. He's the expert coin appraiser who came up to see *the penny*." Cameron added in a chuckle. He looked quite happy this morning.

"Welcome to the bakery, Mr. Lomax." I looked at Cameron. "How did the meeting go?"

"Your cookies were a hit. Only crumbs left by the end of the meeting. Daniel enjoyed them so much, he insisted we stop in for a treat."

"Best chocolate chip and shortbread cookies I've had since I was a boy," Daniel said. "My grandfather used to own a bakery in Washington. It's hard work. I remember him getting up in the middle of the night to bake bread."

"It takes a lot of work, but it's rewarding." Since Cameron

seemed to miss my meaning when I asked about the meeting, I asked it more directly. "What about Rusty's penny?"

Cameron chuckled again. "Oh, that. It's a fake. Worthless."

"Ah, that's a shame," I said. "Rusty seemed so sure he'd found a rare coin."

Cameron took off his hat and smoothed back his thin hair before returning the hat to his head. "Rusty's devastated, of course. I tried to call him this morning, but he wouldn't answer my calls." Cameron seemed far too happy about his friend's misfortune. Competition could make good friends turn sour. "He wouldn't even come out for a walk to the bakery. Oh, but if you could keep this to yourself, please, Scottie. I don't want to be the one spreading news about Rusty's bad luck." It was happening again—people entrusting me with secrets. I was sure this one would spread faster than the initial one. "Daniel insisted on doing the appraisal in private. He's all class." Cameron seemed to have touch of hero worship for his friend.

"You never do important appraisals in front of an audience, like that popular show on television. If the penny had been real and worth a lot of money, then it would be like having Rusty walking around with a million dollars in his pocket. It wouldn't be safe for him or the penny. Besides, I was pretty sure it wouldn't be real, and I wanted to spare the poor man the humiliation."

"That was kind of you," I told Daniel. "And don't worry, I won't tell anyone." More customers streamed into the bakery. "Now what can I get the two of you?"

fourteen

...

JACK and I sat for a break after the morning rush. "I think we should double the amount of Danish on Saturdays," Jack said. "I turned away some disappointed customers this morning. I tried to talk people into the lemon poppy seed and blueberry muffins, but I suppose when you've got your mind set on a sugary Danish, a muffin won't do the trick."

I pulled the notepad over and wrote down the suggestion. It was a good one. "I've been keeping a spreadsheet of data on which treats are big sellers and when. Hopefully, once I have a full year of data, we'll be able to create a more stable product list. Like we noticed a few days ago, the apple Danish lose their appeal once fall and winter are over. It makes sense. Just like with pumpkin, people tire of apple once those seasons have passed.

Jack chuckled. "The fall obsession with pumpkin is one for the history books. Pumpkin spice this and pumpkin butter that. Who would have guessed a round gourd could be such a rock star? By the way, I've got a pumpkin coffee cake recipe up my sleeve that I think will knock everyone's socks off next fall."

"Yum, I can't wait to try that. Seriously, Jack, you are such an asset to this business. Which reminds me, how are you doing on ingredients for the Lady Baltimore cake?"

"Now that you mention it—I was thinking of trying some chopped dried cherries in the filling."

"I thought your filling was delicious," I said.

"It was good, but this cake—it has to be—" He dropped his face. It was something he did when he didn't know how to express himself.

"You want this to be the best cake ever." I patted his hand. "You don't need to prove anything to Crystal Miramont. Trust me, she's not worth the effort. Besides, you are the best baker I've ever had the pleasure to work with. But if you want to try it with cherries, I say go for it. I'm sure Roxi has some dried cherries in the aisle with the nuts and trail mix. I'll walk over to her store and buy some."

"Thanks, Scottie. But you're right. I've got to stop thinking of this as a way to show Miss Miramont that I'm more than a gruff old man with a faded tattoo and an unfortunate past. I'm a good baker, and she's lucky to have me in charge of her Lady Baltimore cake."

"Good attitude. I'll be right back." I untied my apron, grabbed my coat and hurried across to the market. I'd volunteered readily to buy the cherries because I hoped to catch Roxi alone. Now that the morning had slowed, I had more time to process my odd conversation with Dalton. Was he thinking about breaking off the engagement? More importantly, had I said anything that might persuade him one way or another? I sure hoped not. I'd gone over my words in my head a few times. I knew them well because they were the words I used to calm myself whenever I panicked about the decision I'd made. There were a few glum, regret-filled months after I broke it off with Jonathan. For one thing, I hastily purchased a derelict building in the heart of town. It had been the previous town bakery, but it was so far from the lovely, glossy bakery of my dreams that it all seemed impossible. It was buyers' remorse on steroids. But I got through the depression and the bouts of regrets, and once I got things moving on my new life, there was no turning back. All those regrets were long since dead and buried. I'd made the right decision. Last I heard, Jonathan had married a woman his mother introduced him to. They only knew each other a few months. I think his mother was determined to show the world how fabulous she was at planning a wedding. I wished them happiness.

My hurried steps faltered some when I stepped into the store. I was hoping to find Roxi alone for a quick chat, but Amy and Regina were standing at the counter having a lively discussion. Amy looked happy. Was the secret already out or was Cameron a better secret keeper than Rusty? Was Amy in a good mood because she no longer had to fret that she'd sold a million-dollar coin for the price of an old cigar box? Or was it because she was still counting on half the money?

The answer came quickly when I noticed that Amy was

showing Roxi and Regina a full color brochure with a shiny blue Mercedes on the cover. She was listing all the features, so I had to assume she was thinking about buying the car.

I walked to the aisle with nuts and dried fruit and grabbed two bags of cherries off the shelf. I'd gotten to know Jack pretty well, and I was sure he'd try several batches of filling with the cherries before settling on the best one.

Amy and Regina were still at the counter. I was hoping they'd leave. Regina spotted me first. "Scottie, come look at this car Amy is planning to order. It's spectacular."

Amy pushed the brochure at me. I didn't know much about cars, but the model was sleek and sporty, and I was sure it came with a high price tag. "Wow, that's quite a car," I said.

Amy smiled smugly and hugged the brochure against her chest. "It's the car I've always dreamed of driving, and when I get my half of the coin money, I'm going to put in the order. It'll take around six months because I'm going with a custom peach color and ivory leather interior."

"It sure was lucky when Rusty found that coin," Regina said. "I'd love to have a car like that, but I'm afraid I'll only have one in my dreams."

I plastered on a faint smile. I was the only person standing at the counter who knew, without a doubt, that Amy would not be driving that peach-colored Mercedes around town any time soon. I was glad I was sworn to secrecy because I certainly didn't want to be the one to break the news to her. I guess Cameron was a better secret keeper than Rusty, and this time, Rusty wouldn't be quite so keen or anxious to tell everyone his news. I was sure he regretted making such a big deal about it to everyone in town. The poor man would probably be hiding out at home for a few days to avoid the humiliation.

Roxi, who was always far more sensible than most people, spoke up. "I wouldn't order that car just yet, Amy. You told me yourself that you were prepared to hire a lawyer to fight for your half of the money. Rusty might put up a good fight too. Technically, he owns that penny."

Regina had been on the cheer squad side of the Mercedes, but she just as easily slipped to the cold-water side. "That's right, Amy. What's that whole phrase about possession? And there's some fraction that goes with it." It was more of a lukewarm than a cold-water attempt, but Regina made a valid point.

"Possession is nine-tenths of the law," Roxi added helpfully. "That coin is in Rusty's possession."

Amy wriggled indignantly in her coat. "That doesn't matter. He stole that penny from my shop. He owes me my half, and I will hire a lawyer to make sure I get it."

"Don't forget how expensive lawyers are," Roxi said. She was having a little too much fun bursting Amy's luxury car bubble. "My cousins sued each other for their parents' money and property. The lawyers' bills were so high, they were left with very little inheritance."

I rolled my lips in. I could douse the whole conversation with cold water with one short sentence. Amy'd had enough of Roxi's negative comments. She smiled at Regina. "You'll be the first to get a ride around town when this baby gets delivered." She made a point of not making the same promise to Roxi. She swept out of the store with her brochure.

Regina looked askance at the way Amy left the shop. "I don't think she was very happy with us mentioning the possibility of not getting that money."

"Seems that way." Roxi clucked her tongue. "I think that coin might prove more trouble than it's worth to Rusty."

"Not if it's worth a million bucks," Regina said. "What do you think about all of this, Scottie?"

"Me? I think this whole thing will die down faster than you realize."

"I'm not so sure," Regina said. "I hear Henry thinks he's also entitled to half. What a terrible mess—and all because of a penny." It seemed Regina was in no hurry to leave the shop, so I paid for the cherries. I needed to get back to the bakery.

Roxi handed me the cherries and squinted suspiciously at me. She could tell I knew more than I was letting on. Fortunately, she kept that to herself.

"See you gals later," I said. My talk with Roxi would have to wait for another time.

fifteen

. . .

JACK MADE several attempts at a filling with dried cherries, then decided to go back to the last filling he made before the cherry idea. I hated that he was tying himself in knots about this darn cake. I talked Jack into an early lunch. He needed to step away from the mixing bowl for an hour. Traffic in the shop had slowed to the usual late morning crawl. Most of the bread baskets were empty, and a majority of the pastries had been sold. Brownies and cookies were the stars of the afternoon. People came in to buy a treat to go with their lunch.

I was whipping up a batch of chocolate buttercream to top our walnut brownies when the front door opened. I put down the spoon I was holding, wiped off my hands and walked to the front of the shop to help the next customer. My steps faltered when I saw Crystal standing in the center of the bakery. She was wearing a shiny silver coat over a pair of tight leather pants. Even though the coat was puffy, she had her arms crossed tightly in front of her. Nothing about her expression said "I'm dying for a fudge brownie." Her heavily glossed lips were tight with anger.

"Hello, Crystal," I said hesitantly. My woman's intuition told me we weren't about to have a pleasant conversation.

Crystal's eyes flicked toward the kitchen. "Can we talk outside?"

"Nope," I said flippantly to counter her sharp request. "We're alone. Jack is on break, and I'm minding the shop. What can I do for you?" I asked in a business tone. I started to cross my arms like her, then reminded myself that I had no reason to be defensive. She'd put me on guard with her posture and expression and general harshness, but whatever this was about—it was her problem. Not mine.

"First of all, you can quit being so buddy-buddy with my fiancé." She was getting right to the point, and the point was sharp.

I was determined to keep my cool. I had no stakes in whatever she was starting here. "By 'buddy-buddy,' do you mean I should never talk to him, even when he comes in the bakery to buy a pastry?"

"You know exactly what I mean. Look, I know you've been madly in love with Dalton since we were in school. And I'm sorry he never liked you. But that doesn't mean you should be hanging out with him. I suppose showing up at the restaurant last night was a coincidence." She rolled her eyes. Her long lashes flipped up and down like insect wings.

"Cade made the reservation. And yes, it was a coincidence. A very unfortunate coincidence. We were hoping for a quiet dinner, instead we had to listen to you babble on about expensive cakes and satin gloves. Everyone in that restaurant last night now knows you have a ten-thousand-dollar wedding cake."

Her face grew red, and her mouth twisted with anger. I had no idea what brought all this on.

"You're just jealous because I'm rich and beautiful, and I have Dalton and you don't."

"And humble, don't forget humble," I said.

She waved away the sarcasm. "I knew when you decided to settle here that you had more than starting a bakery on your mind. You've been trying to win Dalton over. It's pathetic."

It felt as if I'd traveled back in time. Crystal was acting like a spoiled teenager. It was times like this when I wanted to blurt out my secret, that I was far richer than the Miramont family, but like I'd told Jack—Crystal wasn't worth it.

I looked at her plainly. "Yes, you are rich and beautiful and you have Dalton. And good for you. I have everything I want and I'm happy, and nothing about your life changes that. But I would love to know what brought this tantrum on."

"It's not a tantrum. It's a warning. Stay away from Dalton. Two of my friends were at Roxi's across the street this morning, and they saw Dalton going into the bakery. They said he was the only customer, but he was in here for a long time. How long does it take to put one of those greasy pieces of dough into a bag? And I've been telling him not to eat any more baked goods. I need him looking fit and fine for the wedding photos."

"Dalton came in and bought a cheese Danish. You're in here ranting and raving because the man has a pastry habit?" I was working hard to keep as calm and unaffected by the conversation as possible.

"Oh, please," she said snidely. I realized then that Crystal wasn't all that beautiful, especially when she was snarling mad. "My friends texted me about the incident. You must have said something to him about not getting married."

I laughed. "What incident? Buying a cheese Danish? Your friends either need to get a life or you need better friends because they were clearly trying to upset you. Dalton comes in here most mornings for a pastry. Sometimes I'm at the counter. Sometimes Jack is up front. He buys his treat and leaves." It was true this morning's visit took an interesting turn, but that had all come from Dalton's side. It seemed he was having doubts, and Crystal was sensing it.

She placed her hands firmly on her slim hips. "Then maybe you can explain why Dalton was so cold to me when I called him. After I got the text from my friends, I called to remind him not to eat any more of your calorie-laden garbage before the wedding. Then I brought up a few questions from the caterer, and he cut me off. He said he didn't want to talk about the wedding anymore. He told me to handle the problem and leave him out of it. Just because your man smartly dumped you before the big day doesn't mean you need to get your nose into our business. Dalton and I are getting married this June and then you can cry into your pillow every night. I'll bet you did that a lot back when we were in school."

This was the Crystal I grew up with, the cruel, entitled bully. Dalton had convinced himself that she'd changed, but she was still the same person, only older and meaner. I wondered if Dalton was slowly realizing that. Was that why he was having doubts about the wedding? Crystal was being so harsh, I badly wanted to blurt that out—that Dalton was in the bakery asking how I knew it was time to break it off with Jonathan. But I wouldn't—even though it was never spoken out loud, our conversation was confidential.

"I broke it off with Jonathan, but go ahead and believe what you want about it. None of it matters to me, just like your wedding, your marriage and your relationship with Dalton mean nothing to me. In fact, if you're so confident that it's all taking place this June, then I wonder why you'd bother to come in here and confront me about this. Maybe your intuition tells you something different. And if that's the case, then I'm truly sorry. But none of this has anything to do with me. I won't ban Dalton from the bakery. If you think it's healthy for one person to tell the other where or what they can eat, then go ahead and have that conversation with your fiancé. In the meantime, I'm a business owner, and if a customer comes in to buy one of my goods, then I'm going to sell it to them. That said—if you'd like something I can pack it up for you, otherwise I'm quite busy."

Crystal huffed and puffed a few seconds while she tried to find her next words. "And to think I brought you some business. Thought I'd be helping you out."

I laughed dryly. "Helping me out? By insulting my assistant? I don't need your cake order. We've got more than enough business to handle as it is."

"Fine, then consider my order cancelled. I don't want some creepy ex-convict making my cake. There's a much better bakery up at the resort." She had such a bitter soul. I was relieved that Jack was on his lunchbreak. I only wished we'd shut down the bakery for lunch, so I could have avoided this vile encounter as well.

"I wonder why Ranger Braddock makes a point of driving down here for his cheese Danish," I said.

"You've always been unlikable," Crystal sneered. "You and that freaky hippie grandmother of yours. Just stay away from Dalton." Her heels struck the floor sharply as she walked out of the store.

I practically crumbled in relief after she left. I lifted my hand. It was shaky. It was such an unexpected, unprovoked attack that it left me reeling. I still hadn't recuperated when Jack returned from lunch.

He pointed over his shoulder with his thumb. "I just saw Miss Miramont peel off in her Land Rover as if the devil was chasing her."

I took a deep breath. Jack instantly sensed something was wrong. He hurried across the shop. "You look upset."

I wasn't in the right state of mind to rehash the whole thing yet. "Let's just say, I had an unfortunate run-in with Miss Miramont. And"—I gave him a sympathetic smile—"she cancelled her cake order. But it had nothing to do with you. It was all me."

Jack released a huge sigh. "Thank goodness. I regretted opening my mouth about that cake. But you've got me worried. You look shell-shocked. Why was she here?"

"Now that you ask—I'm not entirely sure. I just hope we've seen the last of her."

sixteen

. . .

IT WAS time for my lunch break, and boy, did I need it. Somehow, I'd become entangled in a rough spot in Dalton's and Crystal's relationship. I wanted nothing more than to be free of the mess. Dalton had talked to Nana about his pre-wedding jitters. I wondered if she'd given advice that leaned too heavily on the breakup side. Right now, she was the only person I wanted to talk to. Nana was a great listener, especially when I was stressed, and there was no other way to describe how I was feeling.

I was just about to get my coat and purse when Daniel Lomax walked into the bakery. He was alone this time. He offered a polite smile. "All morning, I told myself, 'Don't do it, Dan. Don't give in to temptation.' But your baked goods are just too good. I can't explain it, but I think the word I want is bittersweet. Your treats fill me with a bout of home-sickness that makes me miss my grandparents, and at the same time, eating them brings me joyful memories of childhood."

Admittedly, his compliments eased some of the tension I'd been feeling. "That's what we strive for," I said. "How long are you staying in town?"

He laughed. "Well, if I can pull myself away from your pastries, I'll be leaving tomorrow. I promised Cameron that I'd play a few games of chess at the park tomorrow. And this town is so scenic. I don't relish the idea of driving back down the mountain. Cameron has graciously allowed me to use his guest bedroom."

"Was he able to get ahold of Rusty?" I asked. "I haven't seen him all day. He usually stops by for a pastry."

"I think they spoke briefly." Daniel's mouth pulled down. "I felt so bad having to break the news to him. Poor man really thought he'd found a rare coin. But that's the way of it with collecting. There are so many fakes out there, and some of them are really good. It takes a lot of scrutiny and expertise to separate the real from the counterfeit." Daniel patted his stomach as he gazed into the display case. "Let's see. I'll bet that walnut brownie will bring back some good memories. I'll take one please." He grinned. "My heart says two, but my head says one."

"Darn that head," I quipped. "Sometimes the heart knows better." As I said it, something profound struck me, something that helped explain my confusion when it came to Cade. My head was telling me Cade was the one. He was the man I needed for a good relationship. Unfortunately, my heart was still holding on to the feelings I had for Dalton. I needed to get rid of those pesky butterflies. I packed up a brownie and Daniel left.

I hurried to the back and grabbed my things. "I'll be back after lunch, Jack."

"All right. Now that I'm done experimenting with the Lady Baltimore, I can get a head start on measuring ingredients for next week."

"Perfect." I was glad that Jack was relieved not to bake Crystal's cake. Something told me he was losing sleep over the darn thing, and like I'd said many times—she wasn't worth it.

I drove home. Nana had placed a grilled cheese sandwich and salad on the table for me. She was sipping some iced tea and reading a book, waiting for my arrival. My grandmother was so in tune with my feelings, I'd barely taken off my coat when she asked what was wrong.

"Oh, Nana." She stood and I walked straight over to hug her. It instantly made me feel better.

"Come eat and you can tell me all about it." We sat at the table. "Now, what has my Button so worked up? Troubles at the bakery?"

"No, the bakery is fine." I paused to take a few much-needed bites. "It all started this morning when Dalton came in to apologize for Crystal's behavior last night at the restaurant." I'd mentioned a few things about my date with Cade. Naturally, our unfortunate table position came up first. "Then he asked me what it was that made me realize I wasn't going to marry Jonathan."

Nana didn't seem shocked by what I'd said. Instead, she

rolled in her top lip and nodded. "Yes, he asked me what I thought caused you to make that decision. I'm sorry, Button, at the time I might have told him that he'd have to ask you because I wasn't sure what to answer."

"That's all right, Nana. Dalton's visit was confusing, but that's not what turned my day upside-down. This afternoon, after Jack left for lunch, Crystal walked in or, I should say, marched in on pointy heels. We never have great interactions, but this one was positively poisonous. She seems to think I'm trying to steal Dalton, and in very harsh terms, she reminded me why that would never happen. Her friends saw Dalton in the bakery this morning, and I guess because his visit lasted longer than necessary for a pastry purchase, they immediately sent a text to Crystal to let her know."

"Nice friends," Nana said wryly.

"See, that's what I tried to tell her. Apparently, she called Dalton right after and started asking him something about a wedding detail, and Dalton cut her off. Told her he didn't want to deal with anything else about the wedding. And somehow, she's decided that's my fault." It felt good to get all this off my chest, and I'd come to the right person. No one knew me like Nana.

"Poor Dalton. Poor Crystal," she added and then quickly explained. "If this wedding gets cancelled, she'll be devastated."

"That's true. But a big, lavish wedding is never a reason to marry someone you're having doubts about. No one knows that more than me. I think Jonathan was far more upset about not having the big day than about losing me. I know that was the case with his mother."

My emotional side was feeling much lighter after talking with Nana. I finished the sandwich, and Nana made us some coffee. She sat down with her gentle, now-let's-really-talk smile.

I peered at her over my coffee cup. "I think I know what's coming next."

"Button, how are you feeling about all this? I've been sensing Dalton's hesitation for months, and I think I know why he's feeling that way. But you're convinced it has nothing to do with you."

"Because that would be silly. Dalton was engaged to Crystal before I even returned to Ripple Creek. It's true we started our friendship up almost as if we'd never parted, but that's all it is—a friendship. Crystal has all the qualities a man could ask for."

Nana reached over and patted my cheeks. "Except she's not you. Dalton is fond of you. That said—so is Cade. You two have been seeing each other a lot."

"I love hanging out with Cade. My head is telling me he's the right person. But—"

"But your heart belongs to Dalton," Nana finished for me.

"Yes, I think. Ugh, I don't know. I don't allow myself to think about it because—well—Dalton is supposed to get married this summer. And sometimes when I'm with Cade, I'm convinced my heart is with him, too. Sometimes it seems my feelings for Dalton are just leftover edges of that long-held crush. Maybe I need to let those go, then I'll have a solid feeling in my head and my heart." I groaned. "In the meantime, my main focus has to be the bakery. The last thing I need right now is boy troubles."

Nana laughed. "But boy troubles are so much fun."

"I used to think that—back when they were the only important trouble to think about. One thing I know for sure—when I see Crystal Miramont heading my way, I'm turning in the opposite direction. After today—I worry that Dalton has gotten himself into something that is never going to make him truly happy."

"I think you're right, Button."

seventeen

. . .

"I'VE GOT a batch of blueberry muffins in the oven for tomorrow," Jack said as I returned to the shop.

"Great. I think I'll make a few coffee cakes. People like those." I opened the shop on Sunday morning just for muffins and pastries. Jack took Sundays off. I closed by eleven. Monday was my one true day off, however I usually stopped in to catch up on paperwork or make bread starters. I was looking forward to a little downtime. This week had been trying and for all the wrong reasons. My chat with Nana had produced one especially clear conclusion—I needed to focus on my business and leave *boy troubles* behind. I'd been spending way too much time and wasting too much brain energy trying to decipher my relationship with Cade. I'd just go with the flow and let things happen or not happen naturally. And as for Dalton—his troubles with Crystal had nothing to do with me.

The front door opened. "I'll go," I said. I held my breath as I tied on my apron. Crystal's visit had shaken me. I was relieved to find Rusty standing at the counter. He looked how I felt—deflated and glum.

I reached the counter and offered my best sympathetic smile. "I'm sorry, Rusty. I heard about the penny."

His mouth was pulled tight as he nodded. "Yes, well, we'll see."

I was surprised by his response. "Oh, is there still a chance? I heard differently."

Rusty straightened his hunched shoulders. "From who? Cameron, I suppose. He could hardly hide his glee when Daniel claimed it was a fake." It was true. I'd seen the same glee on Cameron yesterday morning.

"What are your next steps?" I asked. "A new appraiser?"

"I'm researching names to find one that's not too far away. I'll accept Daniel's appraisal for now. It helps me in the short term. Henry Voight showed up angry to my house. He knocked so hard I thought the window on the door might break. I told him that Lomax had declared it a fake. Boy, you should have seen his face. It was red, and his mouth twisted like he'd been sucking on a lemon. Henry told me he didn't believe me. He accused me of lying so that I wouldn't have to share the money with him. Then he threatened a lawyer." He pointed to a brownie. "That big one, please."

I reached in and plucked out the big brownie. "I'm sorry to hear all this, Rusty. That penny sure has caused you trouble. It would have been wonderful if the penny had been worth a million dollars, but it'll probably cause you a lot less headaches if it's just a penny."

Right on cue, as if she'd heard our discussion, Amy came bursting into the bakery. "There you are, Rusty. You've been avoiding me. I've called you three times." Amy was hyper and abrasive, but Rusty remained calm. The whole scene reminded me of my encounter with Crystal. Normally, standing inside the bakery brought smiles and joy.

"I haven't been returning any calls, Amy," Rusty said. He patted the phone in his shirt pocket. "I'm not in the mood to talk right now. I just came in to buy a brownie."

"Well, I'm here now, and you can eat your brownie just as soon as you tell me what's going on with that penny." She tapped her foot impatiently.

"Nothing is going on with it. Daniel Lomax, the expert, has declared it a fake." Rusty's shoulders slumped more than usual as he said it.

Amy's face twitched a few times. "You're lying. That's why the three of you did the appraisal in private. You didn't want people to hear the truth. I will have my half of the money."

I'd had enough problems this morning and didn't want to step into this scene, but poor Rusty looked so depressed about the whole thing. Who knew a penny could cause so much havoc?

"Actually, Amy, Daniel Lomax was in here earlier—" I started.

Rusty's face snapped my direction. "He's still in town?"

"Yes, until tomorrow, I think."

Rusty rolled his eyes but didn't elaborate.

"Anyhow, Amy," I continued, "Daniel told me the coin was counterfeit."

Amy was shaking her head. "Of course, he did. They're all in this together. Why else would it have been done in secret?"

Before Rusty could explain, I spoke up. I was already past stepping into the scene. I was right in the middle of it now. "Daniel said he never does important appraisals in front of an audience. It made sense to me. Someone might have tried to steal it from Rusty on his way home." I left off the part about not wanting to humiliate Rusty in front of a crowd. Rusty was already having a bad day.

"I don't believe it," Amy said. She was determined to have that dream car.

Rusty sighed sadly. "I'm afraid it's true, Amy."

Amy lifted her chin. "Well then, if it's not worth anything, you can hand it back to me. It belongs to me anyway."

"Uh—well—uh—it doesn't belong to you," Rusty finally managed to say.

Amy shot me a knowing look. "See, if it's worthless, then why won't he just hand it back to me?" It was hard to argue her point.

"All right." Rusty blew out an exasperated breath. "Daniel Lomax did tell me it was a worthless fake, but I want to make double sure first. I'm researching some coin appraisers in the area. But let me tell you this, Amy, I bought that penny fair and square. If it's genuine, then I'll probably keep it in my collection for now. It'll put me on the map in the collector's world. Everyone will know that I own a 1943 Lincoln copper penny. I'll decide when to sell it, and I won't be sharing any money with you or Henry."

Amy scrunched her face up angrily. "Henry has no part in this. He sold me that penny. It belongs to me."

"And you sold the penny to me," Rusty reminded her.

"Only because I didn't know it was in that cigar box," she countered.

"Just like Henry didn't know it was in the cigar box," Rusty said.

Amy had no good reply. She was using the same defense as Henry.

Jack had walked out to the front to find out what the loud discussion was about. He didn't join in but watched with interest. I had no idea how all of this would end, but I wasn't getting a good feeling about it.

Amy snorted in anger. "So, Henry is in on this too?"

Rusty looked exhausted. His posture took another hit, and it was already poor to begin with. "You're just making up conspiracy theories, Amy. No one is in on anything. Lomax told me officially and in no uncertain terms that the coin was a fake. I'm just planning to get a second opinion, like someone might do with a doctor's diagnosis. Now, I'm going to leave the bakery and eat my delicious brownie. As far as I'm concerned, this discussion is over." He walked a wide berth around Amy.

"You'll be hearing from my lawyer," Amy said as Rusty reached the door. His shoulders slumped even more. He didn't look back or respond. He walked out the door and pushed the brownie into his mouth.

Amy glanced at the cookies and brownies.

"Can I get you anything?" I asked.

She huffed, much the same way Crystal had this morning, and walked out as forcefully as when she walked in.

I turned to Jack. He was holding back a smile.

"I love this town, but sometimes it's the silliest place on earth," I said.

"It does have its share of characters. I feel bad for Rusty," Jack said. "He looked so down; I half expected him to crawl out of here on hands and knees."

"Poor guy. He was so thrilled when he found that penny. Now it's become nothing but a problem."

"Do you think there's anything to it?" Jack asked. "Getting a second opinion, I mean."

"I think he's just not ready to let go of that dream yet. Daniel Lomax spoke confidently about his appraisal. Oh well, I guess this is 'drama central' today. I'll start washing the pans, so I can close up on time. This week has been exhausting. I'm looking forward to some peaceful time off."

eighteen

. . .

I WAS MORE than pleased to flip over the closed sign. Jack had left an hour earlier, and aside from a few customers buying cookies, the store was quiet. I finished cleaning and headed into my office to do some paperwork. My phone buzzed with a text as I sat down at my desk. It was from Dalton.

"I'm at the bakery door. I saw a light on in the back, so I decided to text."

I got up and hurried to the door. Crystal had left me with a good dose of paranoia. It seemed she had spies around town watching and waiting to report back to the queen. I opened the door and looked past Dalton across the street. He looked behind him in confusion. "Are you expecting someone?" he asked. Then his face smoothed. "Oh, you're waiting for Rafferty."

I looked at him. "What? No." I shook my head in aggravation, grabbed his hand and yanked him into the shop before shutting the door.

Dalton glanced outside again. "Now you're freaking me out. Why are you acting so weird?" He was wearing a hint of a smile as he asked it. I was about to burst his amused bubble.

"I'm not acting weird, but maybe you should talk to your fiancée. Apparently, she has friends who are tracking your moves, particularly when your moves lead my direction."

Dalton's smile disappeared. "What are you talking about?"

For all of a second, I considered not mentioning my visit from Crystal, but I couldn't be caught up in this anymore. I motioned for him to follow me back to the kitchen. It was too easy to see into the front of the shop. I'd planned it like that so people passing by would glance in and see the piles of delectable treats and come inside. What I hadn't planned was for my big front windows to become a spying tool for Crystal's team of stalkers. (Granted, that might be an exaggeration, but I didn't want to take a chance.)

My stealthy relocation to the kitchen had Dalton even more confused. "Seriously, Scottie, what's going on?"

"Tea?" I asked as I waved to a stool.

"No. I think I need to hear this standing up because something tells me I'm not going to like it."

"Crystal came to see me this morning. Here, in the bakery."

Dalton's chest rose and fell with a deep breath. His brown eyes grew darker. "What happened?"

"I really don't have the stomach to rehash all of it, but

apparently, her friends saw you in the bakery this morning. They decided you were in here for far too long, so they texted Crystal about it—she called it an 'incident.'"

Dalton was shaking his head. "That's Tammy and Violet. They're always trying to stir up trouble. I told Crystal they weren't good friends." He looked at me. "Was it bad? What did she say?"

I should have told him all the details, and maybe then he'd realize that Crystal hadn't changed. She was still the same unlikable girl we grew up with. She was still the same girl who laughed when Kelly Thurgood tripped over her untied shoelaces and fell face first into her lunch tray. She was still the same girl who made a big show of inviting only her "loyal and special" friends to her carnival-themed birthday party. There were actual rides and animals and games with prizes. Of course, she shared photos of the event to all us poor saps who'd been left off the invite list. But I was resolved to not get any further into this. Dalton would have to open his eyes and see it for himself.

He might have wanted to stay standing, but I found I needed the support of the stool beneath my bottom. What I was about to say wasn't going to be easy… especially for me. I sat down. He decided to sit, too. The profound worry on his face was sweet, and I resisted the urge to place my palm against his cheek.

"I think it would be best if you and I didn't—if we didn't hang out. Maybe you should try the bakery up by the resort." My words slammed against him. I hadn't expected him to look so hurt by my suggestion.

"What are you saying? You don't want me to come around here or your house anymore? I thought we were friends."

"We are and nothing can change that, but you're going to be married soon. You'll be busy as Crystal's new husband."

His jaw tightened. "What did she say to you? She did this, didn't she? Crystal is trying to control every aspect of my life. That was why I asked you those questions this morning. I know Jonathan was trying to control you, too. I don't—I can't live like that."

"Have you told her that? Seems like this is a discussion you should be having with Crystal."

He laughed dryly. "Have you met her? She's not great at taking criticism or orders. But if she came in here with threats and telling you not to talk to me anymore, then she's crossed that final line. We're going to have a discussion, and this time she's going to have to listen."

Before he could hop up and take off for his discussion, I took his hand. "First of all, do not tell her you spoke to me. In fact, promise me that my name will not come up at all. Leave the bakery out of it, too." Just like Rusty's posture, Dalton's face fell with each word. "And secondly, I think what I suggested earlier will help smooth things out between you. I don't want to be the cause of this rough spot."

Dalton raked his fingers through his hair. "I can't believe this. So, I'm supposed to give up my friends for her? Sounds like a bang-up way to start a marriage."

"Not all your friends, surely. Just me. I seem to be the one on her radar. She never liked me much."

"Do you know why?" he asked.

I shrugged. "I always avoided her in school, but that didn't stop her from saying mean things to me."

"That's because she knew *I* liked you. She asked me to take her to the sixth-grade spring dance, but I told her no because I wanted to ask you. Then I got sick with the flu, so I never got a chance. A few months later we were packing up the house."

I was glad I'd decided to sit. The wind had been knocked out of me, and I was blinking at him in utter disbelief. "That can't be true," I finally croaked out.

"It's all true."

How badly I wanted to spill everything, the crush, the tears and heartbreak when he left town, the whole darn soap opera that had been my teen years. I had to swallow his glorious but heartbreaking confession and keep it tucked away for good. "Dalton, you're going to be married soon. We'll revisit our friendship at another time. Right now, you need to concentrate on Crystal and your future, and I need to focus on the business." There was that terrible look of hurt again. How did he make it look so darn appealing?

"So that's it? You're just going to let Crystal bully you into severing our friendship?"

"Don't think of it that way, Dalton. The woman you love and plan to marry has made it clear she doesn't want me involved in your life. While I'm not happy about it, I think this is for the best. I don't need any more grief from Crystal. You two need to work all this stuff out before the wedding." I stood up. So did he, reluctantly. He gazed at me for a long time, long enough that I almost withdrew the whole plan, long enough to put a lump in my throat.

"Fine, I guess I'll take my bakery business elsewhere. I need to cut down anyhow." His words were curt. He headed out of the kitchen and continued to the door. He stopped before walking out and turned back to me. "Would you have said yes?" he asked. "If I hadn't gotten sick before the dance, would you have said yes?"

Inside my head I was laughing hysterically. Had he really not known that I was bonkers about him? I cleared my throat. "Uh yeah, I probably would have said yes."

My answer pleased him. "Wish I hadn't gotten sick," he said as he opened the door. He looked back once more and then walked out.

"Me, too, Dalton Braddock. Me, too."

I walked back to the office feeling more than a little numb about the conversation. Had I done the right thing? He looked so hurt. But it needed to be done. Crystal made it clear she didn't want me to be part of his life. But if I had done the right thing—why did I feel so crummy about it?

My phone beeped. It was a text from Cade. Probably the last thing I needed at the moment. I picked up the phone and read the text. "In an act of supreme procrastination, instead of writing my next chapter, I've been intensely watching a standoff between a blue jay and a squirrel over a peanut. The squirrel won—if you were curious about the ending."

I laughed and wrote back. "Thank you, Cade, for always putting a smile on my face, even when I'm feeling glum."

"Uh oh," he wrote back. "Do you need a glass of wine and a sympathetic ear?"

"I do, but what I need more is a long bath and an early bedtime. Maybe tomorrow."

"Wish granted." That was all he wrote. He was an expert at knowing exactly what to say.

nineteen
. . .

I'D SLEPT WELL for the first few hours and then spent the rest of the night tossing and turning. I tried hard not to think about the encounter with Crystal or the difficult follow-up conversation with Dalton. The talk with Dalton was the part that kept me up the most. My mind went back and forth between anger at myself for caving to Crystal's demands and telling myself I did the right thing. But as I stood in the bakery surrounded by delicious trays of baked goods, I felt sad knowing Dalton wouldn't be walking in the door. He usually came in moments after I flipped the sign.

After a small flurry of customers, I decided to treat myself to one of Jack's blueberry muffins and a cup of hot coffee. I was enjoying my break when the front door opened. Cade was wearing a black sweater and jeans. The black made his hazel eyes look green. Sometimes Cade looked so handsome, it was as if he'd just stepped off a painter's canvas. And he was wearing my favorite cocky half-smile. I paused to see if there were any butterflies, but they were quiet.

"You're up and about quite early, Mr. Rafferty. Any more intrigue in the squirrel and blue jay saga?"

"No, but I was feeling just cheeky enough to put a handful of cereal on the patio to see if I could rekindle yesterday's drama."

"All in the name of procrastination?"

"Sadly, yes. Do you know there is quite a pecking order in nature?"

"I've heard that, yes. You're like a regular David Attenborough now, it seems."

"I think I prefer Tarzan." Cade pushed the sleeves of his sweater back. He had nice forearms to go with the rest of him.

I laughed.

He patted his stomach. "My refrigerator is close to empty, and I made a pot of coffee only to realize I had nothing to go with it. I'd like two blueberry muffins. I'm hoping they'll inspire me to write that chapter."

I put two muffins in a bag and waved off payment. "On the house. Anything to help a struggling writer."

Cade's smile faded some. "You sounded a little lost yesterday when I texted you."

"It was kind of a rough day, but I'm determined to put it behind me."

"Well, I'm chained to a keyboard this morning, but maybe we can meet up later."

"I'd like that."

Cade lifted the bag with the muffins. "Thanks for the inspiration."

"Just don't feed them to the squirrels," I said as he walked out.

Two more customers came in a few minutes later. Ronald and Dick had lived in Ripple Creek for years. They were two of the regular chess players down at the park. "Well, it's rude for them not to at least call. They said they'd be at the park for the first round of games," Ronald was saying as they stepped inside.

"Morning, guys," I said. "Trouble at the chess tables?"

Dick straightened his cap. "We were expecting Cameron and his friend, Daniel, to show up, but no sign of them. Rusty was also a no-show, and no one is answering their phones. Not very good manners."

"I agree. A phone call doesn't take that long," I said. "I know Rusty is a little out of sorts, but Daniel came into the bakery yesterday. He mentioned he was staying in town an extra day, so he could play chess."

"That's right. Cameron was bragging that his friend was quite the player," Ronald said. "Maybe Daniel was exaggerating his expertise, so he decided not to play and embarrass himself."

Dick nodded. "That's probably right. Wouldn't be the first time someone crowed about their chess skills. Remember Trent's friend—what was his name—Blair or Blaze or something like that? He was in town visiting, and he bragged to all of us that he'd played in some big tournaments, and he didn't think it would be fair to sit down with us. Ronnie finally talked him into a match."

Ronald laughed. "I had his queen before his bottom even warmed the bench. Four moves later, it was checkmate and Blaine, I think that was his name," Ronald looked up at me. "Who names their kid 'Blaine'? Anyway, Mr. Tournament slumped away in complete humiliation, muttering something about the noisy park being too distracting and the sun in his eyes." Ronald's phone rang. He pulled it out of his pocket and rolled his eyes. "Here we go." He answered. "Well, Cameron, what happened? We've been waiting for you since nine." He put it on speaker so that Dick could hear the excuse.

"I apologize, Ronnie. As you know, I have a houseguest, and we stayed up late watching a movie. Slept right through the alarm."

Both men were shaking their heads at the lame excuse. "Bet you had a few too many beers with that movie," Dick said.

"Is that you, Dick?" Cameron asked. "Sorry. We can head over there now. Daniel is just getting out of the shower. He'd still like to play a few rounds."

Ronald looked at Dick. Dick nodded. "We'll see you at the park soon." Before he put his phone away, he scrolled through the screen. "I'm going to try Rusty one more time. I think he'd like to be the person to challenge Cameron's friend. After all, Daniel told him his penny was worthless." He placed the phone to his ear, waited and then left a message. "Hey, Rusty, where are you? We've got some chess to play. Call me when you get this." He hung up. "He must still be stewing about that coin. It's not like him to miss a Sunday game."

"I'm sure he'll come around soon," I said. "Now, what can I get you boys?"

Ronald rubbed his chin as he surveyed the goodies. "That coffee cake looks like it'll hit the spot. I'll take a slice of that and one blueberry muffin."

"I think I'll have the same," Dick said. "Going to need energy if I face off against Cameron's friend, Daniel."

I packed their treats and sent them on their way. As they walked out, I happened to glance through the front window. Dalton was driving past in his ranger's truck. He worked every other Sunday. He glanced toward the bakery, and for the briefest second, our gazes caught. He looked away quickly. It stung, but it was understandable. Nana and I had spoken about everything except men at the dinner table last night. She sensed that I was dealing with some heartbreak and decided not to bring up Dalton or Cade. I never even mentioned Dalton's stunning confession that he was planning to ask me to the spring dance. It was nice talking about other things for a change. She was determined to plant a vegetable garden this summer, and I was all for it. There was nothing like garden-grown tomatoes and beans.

Dalton's truck turned toward the park. I released the breath I'd been holding. How on earth were we going to avoid each other?

This town was too darn small.

twenty
· · ·

ESME DROPPED in as I finished cleaning up. "You're in luck, I have two pieces of coffee cake left," I said. "Would you like some with a cup of coffee?"

"I was hoping you'd say that and yes, I would." Like me, Esme tended to close shop early on Sundays. In the summer, we'd probably have to change that pattern, but right now, while the air was still too cold for rafting down the river and biking along the trails, the shorter hours made sense. It gave both of us a chance to relax and regroup, something I desperately needed this week.

We sat in the kitchen with our slices of coffee cake and cups of coffee. Esme was tall and thin, and her legs folded up like a grasshopper's as she perched on the stool. She took a bite of cake. "Hmm, so good. Oh, I forgot to tell you"—she paused in thought—"I guess it's because we didn't see each other yesterday. Crystal Miramont came into the bookshop.

She stops in sometimes just to drink the free herbal tea." She shook her head. "Rich people are always big on freebies. She likes to look at the wedding idea books. I mean isn't that wedding already planned? She's obsessed with her big day. I was never one of those girls," she said.

"What girls? The ones who had their weddings planned before they even got their braces off? I wasn't, either."

"So, Crystal was in the store sipping my new peppermint tea and thumbing through a book about wedding décor. She's never super-friendly, and she's devoid of charm, but she was particularly ornery yesterday. The cats never go near her, of course. They all skittered out of the reading area when she sat down on the couch. I asked her a question about her flower choices, and she told me she didn't want any of her wedding details to get out because people would try and copy her." Esme laughed. It blew a few crumbs off her napkin. She swept them back up. "Can you imagine having that kind of ego? Yes, everyone is sneaking around trying to find out if she's going to use roses or peonies in her bouquet. Anyway, apparently, I'd annoyed her because she snapped shut the book, tossed it on the coffee table and stormed out. She left her tea on the table too. Very rude."

"She does have rudeness down to an art. I'm sorry. I think her bad attitude might have something to do with me."

Esme's eyes rounded. "Did something happen?"

A siren stopped our conversation. I got up to look out the front window. Dalton's truck raced past.

"Uh oh, looks like our peaceful Sunday has been disrupted," Esme said.

I got up to put my cup in the sink. "I hope it's not anything too terrible." The siren echoed off the mountainside as it left the center of town and headed down one of the side streets.

Esme laughed. "I can see that twinkle in your eye. What if it's a murder scene? We can't have Ripple Creek's best sleuth sitting here in her bakery when there's a killer on the loose."

"It's probably just an accident or a car break-in. Still—maybe I'll head that direction to find out what's going on." I grabbed my coat.

Esme picked up the rest of her coffee cake. "Far be it from me to stand in the way of truth and justice."

I walked out with her and locked the door. "I'm done for the day. How about you?" I asked.

"Yep. Gonna round up my furballs and head home. Have a good day off."

"You, too."

I walked to my car and sat behind the wheel. I was ready to swing the car around and drive in the direction of the siren when something struck me. I told Dalton we needed to avoid each other, and here I was, literally following him. "What are you doing, Scottie? Just turn around and go home," I told myself. In the distance, I heard a second siren. It was coming up the highway at a fast pace. This was more than a break-in. I could always just drive by to check things out. I wouldn't have to talk to Dalton at all.

I swung the car around and headed out of town. The second siren, an ambulance, had reached the road just ahead of me. It was a small dead-end street with a few houses on each side. Dalton's truck was stopped in front of Rusty Simmer's house. The ambulance stopped there, too.

I drove to the end of the road and turned my car around. Dalton was inside the house, and the front door was open. A few concerned neighbors were standing in their front yards. I waited. The paramedics unloaded their gear and a gurney and headed into the house. They were in there for a few minutes. I saw Sally Jenkins, who used to take art lessons from Nana when I was young. She was Rusty's neighbor on the right. She rubbed her hands in distress as she waited for word from the house.

Ronald and Dick said that Rusty never showed for chess, and he wasn't answering his phone. At the time I hadn't thought anything about it. I knew Rusty was still distraught about the penny appraisal. But what if he hadn't gone to chess because he was sick or hurt?

I got out of the car and walked across to Sally's front yard. She was watching Rusty's house and hadn't seen me walk up. "Sally, hello," I said quietly, not wanting to startle her. It took her a few seconds to recognize me. She was an occasional bakery customer. She loved lemon poppy seed muffins.

"Scottie, hello. I didn't see you walk up." She wrung her hands together again. "You'll have to excuse me. I'm in a state of shock. It's just dreadful."

"What's going on? Has something happened to Rusty?"

"Yes, oh Scottie, you should see his house. And poor Rusty. I think he might be—" She shook her head. "I won't say it. Hopefully, the paramedics can do something."

"Is Rusty hurt? What happened to his house?" I glanced

over to Rusty's small green cottage. It was the same size and style as Nana's. From here, everything seemed to be in place.

Sally was still wringing her hands. I took hold of them to calm her. "Is he hurt?"

She nodded. "There was a lot of blood." A sob made her entire body shudder. "It was just horrible. Like a bad movie. Rusty usually comes over to my house for a cup of coffee and a chat on Sunday morning. He never showed up, and he didn't answer my calls. I knew he was upset about that darn penny. Such a shame. I decided to check on him. We keep a copy of each other's house keys in case of an emergency."

"That's a good idea." I released her hands. Talking about the incident seemed to help her calm down.

"I hadn't needed the key at all. The front door was unlocked. I'm afraid we're all careless about locking doors around here." She started fidgeting with the edge of her sweater. I let her. She seemed to need it. "I won't be anymore. None of us are safe in our homes."

"I'm sure that's not the case, Sally."

Sally looked past me. "Oh look, here come the paramedics. Now they can take him to the hospital."

We both watched, anxious to see them roll the gurney into the house. Instead, they rolled it back to the ambulance.

Sally sobbed again. "That's not a good sign," she said weakly.

I patted her arm. "I'm afraid not."

We waited as they loaded up and drove off in the ambulance.

"Does that mean he's dead?" Sally asked. "Or maybe he's

fine." She shook her head. "No, I'm fooling myself. I think I'll go back inside."

I walked Sally to her door and saw that she got in safely. I turned toward Rusty's house and took a deep breath. Here I was breaking my new arrangement with Dalton before it was twenty-four hours old. I should have added an addendum that excluded murder scenes. Of course, maybe Rusty had fallen and hit his head. But Sally had mentioned something about the condition of his house. I'd worried that coin would cause Rusty big headaches. I just hadn't known how big.

Well, I wasn't going to get answers standing out in the yard. I took another deep breath and headed inside. The entry hall closet was open, and Rusty's coats, hats and snow gear were in a pile on the floor. I turned the corner and found Dalton crouched down next to Rusty's body. Rusty looked limp and pale, and his head rested in a pool of blood. The bookshelves on the far side of the room had been emptied, the contents thrown on the floor. A quick survey of the front room and the kitchen showed the same chaotic mess. Someone had ransacked the house.

I took a step and the floor creaked. Dalton looked up quickly, his hand on his gun belt. His shoulders relaxed. "Scottie, it's you." He looked down at Rusty. "Looks like someone killed Rusty Simmer. Seems they were looking for something. There isn't a drawer or cupboard left untouched."

"The penny," I said quietly.

Dalton pushed to his feet. "I've been hearing a lot about the rare penny. Do you think that's what this is all about?"

"I'd bet a million bucks on it."

Dalton pulled out his phone. He stopped and looked at me. "I thought we're supposed to avoid each other."

"Yes, I forgot to put in the exclusion for murder scenes. And I feel like I should have seen this one coming. If this did have to do with the penny, then there are a few people on the suspect list."

Dalton nodded. "Guess it's time to call the coroner."

twenty-one
. . .

WHILE DALTON WAS on the phone with the county coroner, I crouched down next to Rusty. It took me a second to regain my composure. Just yesterday, Rusty was nibbling one of my brownies, and today, he was on the floor, dead in a pool of his own blood. His face was ashen gray. There was a deep wound on the back of his head, but no other signs of injury. A dark blue terry cloth robe was cinched around his waist. He was wearing a pair of green and white flannel pajamas. A suede bedroom slipper dangled from one foot. I glanced around and spotted the edge of the second slipper. It was wedged under the couch. The blood was in just one location. Rusty fell where he was struck, and whoever hit him made sure it was a fatal blow.

Dalton put his phone away. He pulled latex gloves out of his pocket, smiled and handed them to me before taking out another pair for himself. There was no way to deny that things felt a bit awkward, but we had to push that aside for now. Poor Rusty Simmer was dead, and someone needed to be brought to justice.

I pulled on the gloves. They were loose, but they'd do the trick. "In my unprofessional opinion, I'd say he was struck in the head and fell right where he stood. The other slipper is wedged under the couch. It must have flown off when he fell."

"Pretty good for a nonprofessional. I concluded the same thing." Dalton glanced around at the mess in the room. "At first I considered robbery as the motive, but his television, his laptop, even his coin collection were left behind." He tilted his head toward the small hallway off the front room. "I had a look around his office. Same mess. Everything pulled out and turned upside down."

"They were searching for something," I said. "And my money would be on that darn penny. Poor Rusty. He was so excited when he found that coin. What do you think the murder weapon might have been?" I asked.

"No idea, but something heavy. All it took was one blow."

"I spoke to Sally Jenkins a few minutes ago," I said. "She's very distraught."

Dalton nodded. "She made the call. I plan to talk to her after this."

"She told me that Rusty didn't always lock his door, and even though she walked over with a key to check on him, the door was unlocked."

"I doubt a killer would take the time to lock it behind him as he fled the scene."

"Good point," I said. "I guess that's why you have the shiny badge."

"Yeah, lucky me," he muttered. There was more to unpack from his response, but we didn't have time now. We were standing in the middle of a grisly murder scene.

"What if Rusty let the person inside because he knew them?" I said.

"That's a definite possibility. There was no sign of a struggle, and the wound is on the back of his skull. I don't think Rusty saw this coming. If Sally says Rusty doesn't always lock his door, then the attacker might have just walked inside. I'm always telling Evie she needs to lock her door."

I shrugged. "She is from the peace, love and flower-power generation. She says 'If one of my neighbors needs something so badly they need to break in to my house, then I'd rather just let them come in and take it.'"

Dalton shook his head. "She does have a healthier outlook on humanity than most of us."

"Is it all right if I look around?" I asked.

His eyes glittered with amusement. "That's why I handed you the gloves. I knew you'd want to get involved. I'm going to search for a possible murder weapon. Why don't you do the same but out in the yard. It had to be something solid and heavy enough to kill a man with one blow. Seems like something a fleeing killer would want to get rid of quickly."

I nodded. For a second our gazes got caught. I expected things to be strained between us. Instead, things felt surprisingly normal.

I stepped outside and zipped up my coat. Clouds had

moved in to blot out any warmth the sun provided. We weren't out of the woods yet for a late spring snowstorm, and the clouds seemed to be reminding us of that. Rusty's front yard was still brown and leafless from the long winter. It made searching for a murder weapon easy. I glanced inside some of the shrubs. Tiny green buds dotted the branches. They were waiting for the longer hours and warm weather to burst open for summer. No weapon.

Sally came out of her house. She had more color in her face and was dressed for the weather with a coat, gloves and a knit beanie. Her small dog, a poodle mix, was at her side. She waved me over. The dog barked sharply when he saw the stranger approaching.

She glanced down at the dog. "Quiet, Chester." The dog stopped barking and stared at me, wagging his tail. "What are you looking for?" Sally asked. A look of horror crossed her face. "Could the person who did this still be in the neighborhood?"

"Not likely, Sally. Just looking for anything the person might have left behind." I decided not to use the phrase "murder weapon." Sally was already shaken enough.

"I came out here to tell you something that might be important. Last night, I'd gone to bed just after the ten o'clock news. I like to listen to the weather report. That Jack Crescent is such a wonderful weatherman." Sally blushed lightly. It seemed she liked to watch Jack Crescent for more than his weather predictions. "I was fast asleep when Chester jumped off the bed and ran to the front window. He was barking wildly at something. I assumed it was a bear. You know how active and hungry they are after hibernation. James and Katy, at the end of the street, had their trash cans rummaged through just two nights ago. That darn bear pulled everything out of the cans. Such a mess. Anyhow, I called Chester back to bed. Now I'm thinking maybe it wasn't a bear. Maybe Chester heard the intruder at Rusty's house."

"That's possible. Do you happen to know what time that was?"

She nodded with a pleased grin. "I sure do. I have a clock on my nightstand, and it was 12:25. Do you think that's important?"

"I do. Ranger Braddock is going to walk over to talk to you once he's done here. He'll want to hear all about that."

Another smile. "Oh, my, Ranger Braddock." Another blush, possibly even deeper than the Jack Crescent blush. "I better straighten up my kitchen and put on a pot of coffee." As she said it, her posture deflated. "I can't believe Rusty and I aren't going to have our morning talks anymore."

"I'm sorry about that, Sally." Her mention of the bear in the trash had given me an idea. "Sally, do you know where Rusty keeps his trash can?"

"I think it's on the other side of the house. I keep mine in the garage during bear season. Well, I better head inside and straighten up my kitchen if I'm going to have a visitor." She turned and headed back across her yard. Chester followed at her heels.

If there hadn't been a bear in the neighborhood, then Chester might have been barking because he heard Rusty's attacker tearing the house apart. That would put the murder at some time past midnight. Most people would be fast asleep by then, and Rusty certainly looked ready for bed. Had he pulled on his robe to answer a midnight knock at the door? Or had he heard the culprit going through his things? Maybe he went out to confront them.

I circled to the side of the house. Rusty's garbage can was sitting against the side wall between a wheelbarrow and bag of potting soil. It seemed Rusty had plans to start his spring gardening chores. I opened the lid on the trash can. I was glad to have the pair of gloves, even if they didn't fit well. I moved aside a white trash bag that was filled and tied up, and there it was, sitting on top of another bag of trash that was smeared with blood. The killer didn't go through too much effort to hide the wrench. I took a photo of it in the trash can and then pulled it free with just my finger and thumb pinched around the handle end. It was heavy and solid, the perfect tool for cracking someone's head open.

I stepped around to the front of the house just as Dalton came out through the front door. His eyes rounded when he saw what I was holding.

"You found it." He looked impressed.

"It was in the trash can on that side of the house. There's blood on the wrench-y end of it. That's my technical term for the side that grabs and pinches."

"Sounds good to me." He came down the steps and got a closer look at the wrench hanging from my fingers. "Only this time, the wrench-y side was use to break through a human skull. It's a nice one. Exeter brand tools are expensive." The word Exeter was molded into the metal along the handle.

"Find anything of interest other than a mess inside the house?" I asked.

"Nothing of note. Would you happen to know anything about the coin that had everyone up in arms? There are coins in the office, but I don't know what I'm looking for."

I smiled. "Well, then you're lucky I stopped by, Ranger Braddock, because I happen to know a little something about that penny."

twenty-two

DALTON LED me into the small room that Rusty had set up as an office, complete with bookshelves (mostly emptied by the attacker), a desk and a computer. A mahogany wood storage cabinet stood in the corner with its doors hanging open. Like the bookshelves, it had been mostly emptied of its contents. There were folders with pages of coins filed in pockets and sorted by date and denomination. A leather folder contained old silver dollars.

Dalton picked it up. "I'm sure if robbery had been the only motive, then the thief would have, at the very least, taken these old silver dollars."

"I agree. I think robbery was the motive, but it was for one special coin." I sifted through the coins on the floor. Some had come loose from their collector's folder, and others had spilled out of a tin box.

"Are we really looking for a penny?" Dalton asked.

"Yes, it's a 1943 penny. Rusty was sure he'd found a 1943 Lincoln copper penny. There are only thirty or forty in existence."

Dalton looked puzzled. "Why would they only produce thirty or forty pennies that year? I know pennies aren't worth much nowadays, but back then, when a loaf of bread cost nine cents, I would have thought pennies were an important form of currency."

"I'm sure you're right, and they produced plenty of pennies that year, but because of the war, copper was a precious resource. They switched to steel pennies, but a few copper ones were cast by mistake. According to Rusty and his coin buddies, a real 1943 Lincoln copper penny could be worth up to a million dollars."

"Unbelievable." We both crouched down to sift through the coins. It didn't take long to search for a 1943 penny because there were only a handful of pennies in Rusty's collection. "I don't see it," I said.

Dalton put the last penny into the pile with the other coins. "Nope, 1963. I guess the killer got what he was looking for."

"Or Rusty has it hidden somewhere special," I said. "I'm not sure if I'd leave a million-dollar coin sitting in this cabinet."

"True. It's crazy to think something so small and usually insignificant could be worth such a fortune."

"That's just it," I said. "Daniel Lomax is an expert coin

appraiser. He came to town to see the penny and determine whether or not it was the real deal. He told Rusty it was a fake. Rusty didn't want to take his word for it, but I talked to Daniel and he confirmed what he'd told Rusty. The coin wasn't worth anything. But Rusty was so sure he'd found a rare coin, he wasn't ready to accept Daniel's assessment."

Dalton's phone beeped with a text. He pulled it out and looked at it. "The coroner is about five minutes away." We both stood up and, because of the cramped room and the clutter, ended up nearly toe-to-toe. Flustered, I stepped back too quickly and tripped over some fallen books. Dalton caught my hand and kept me from landing on my bottom. He held it even after I'd regained my footing. His dark lashes shadowed his cheeks as he stared down at my hand in his.

I cleared my throat. "Uh, I should probably go since the coroner is on his way." I pulled my hand away as he dropped his grasp. I nearly repeated the pitch backward over the books.

"Right, yeah, uh, yeah, you should go."

We stepped over the clutter and landed in the small hallway, another too close for comfort space. I sidled out first and made it to the front room. Seeing Rusty reminded me of my chat with Sally.

"You need to talk to Sally Jenkins next door," I said. "Her dog started barking wildly just after midnight. It might be related. Oh, and expect to stay for a bit. She's straightening her kitchen and fixing a pot of coffee. She was definitely blushing as she talked about your impending visit."

Dalton sighed. "Such is the life of a small-town ranger. I'll go see her once the coroner gets set up."

We walked to the door and out onto the stoop. "Thanks for your help, Scottie. You always know the important nuances and dynamics that are going on between the people in town. Sometimes I feel like I'm on the outside of town looking in. You're in the heart of it."

"Having the bakery does keep me in the thick of things. Even when I don't want to be in it," I said pointedly.

Dalton's face dropped. "I'm sorry about Crystal's visit, Scottie." He looked at me. "And by the way, I had toast at home. I know other pastries can't compete with yours. Not even worth the drive up to the resort."

"That's nice to hear. Later, I can tell you more about the rifts that penny has caused in town, but I'll let the officials do their thing first. It's the least I can do since I cruelly denied you your Danish this morning."

The coroner van drove around the corner.

Dalton wasn't ready to send me off yet. "You mentioned there were some possible suspects. If this is declared a murder, which will no doubt be the case, who else should I talk to besides Sally Jenkins? I suppose if this has something to do with the penny, then I should start with the members of the coin club."

"Cameron Burke is the president. He's Rusty's good friend, and he brought in Daniel Lomax, the coin expert. But there's another part to the story. It involves how Rusty ended up with the coin."

The coroner and his team were getting out of the van. "I'm

going to need to talk to them. I'll call you later to hear more about the other part of the story."

"All right."

He paused before leaving the stoop. He looked back at me with those dreamy brown eyes, and his right cheek dimple made an appearance. "Does that mean I'm no longer banned from the bakery?"

I groaned at how soft I was when it came to Dalton Braddock. "Just don't tell you-know- who. In fact, make sure to hide napkins and crumbs and any evidence that might lead back to me."

"Got it. Thanks for your help." He hurried out to meet the coroner. I walked across the yard to my car. I sat behind the wheel for a moment watching Ranger Braddock in action. He was smooth and confident, and we were lucky to have him. At the same time, he was lucky to have me. I had some good insider information on this case, and he was once again going to need me, like his woman-on-the-ground reporter. I'd somehow managed to be on the inside of this whole debacle from the beginning. I was in the antique store when Rusty spotted the coin and bought the cigar box. And now, here I was at the terrible, tragic conclusion of the coin saga.

I was off for the rest of the day. Amy's store was open on Sundays. The antique store would be my first stop. That was where this whole thing began, in the back of Amy's shop.

My phone beeped. It was Cade.

"The cereal didn't work. A group of nosy, bossy pigeons landed on my patio and ate every last bit of it. The good news is I wrote five hundred words. To celebrate, I think you should come over for dinner. I'll order in."

"Sounds good," I wrote back.

"Are you still at work?" he asked.

"Nope, I'm at a murder scene."

"That was going to be my next guess," he responded.

"I'll tell you about it later. See you tonight."

twenty-three
· · ·

GRISLY MURDER SCENE OR NOT, I realized I was hungry. I stopped home for a quick bite to eat. Hannah and Nana were sitting on the front couch with cups of tea. After this week, I looked forward to those years when I could just hang out with a friend, shoot the breeze and sip herbal tea. I was curious if word had gotten around about the tragedy. News traveled fast in Ripple Creek, and emergency vehicles followed by the coroner's van would certainly get the ball rolling fast. My question was answered quickly.

Nana looked up from her tea as I walked in. She nearly spilled it as she sat urgently forward. "Have you heard the news, Scottie?"

"It's just horrible," Hannah added. She tended to be over-dramatic, but this time I had to agree with her. It was horrible. Rusty was a kind man who'd spent his harmless, gentle days playing chess and collecting coins. He certainly didn't deserve such a terrible end.

I sat down in the big, comfy chair next to the sofa. When I was young and it was cold outside, I'd pull the quilt from my bed, wrap it around myself like a cocoon and settle down in the chair to do my homework. Nana used to call it my nest.

"Rusty Simmer is dead," I said.

Both women sat up as if I was telling them something new. "So, it's true," Nana said. "You know how stories can grow like wildfires in this town. I remember when Eugene Grant, over on Juniper Lane, injured his foot. By the time the rumor mill swept through town people were shaking their heads in dismay talking about poor Eugene losing his leg below the knee, and weren't they all shocked when Eugene showed up at the farmer's market with a bandaged toe and his entire leg intact."

"I'm afraid this time it's more than a rumor."

"How did it happen?" Hannah asked.

"I'm going to wait for official word from Dalton about this." Both women had this annoying habit of smiling coyly whenever the name Dalton came out of my mouth.

"You spoke to Dalton?" Nana asked. She knew that I'd told Dalton it would be better if we kept our distance. She'd all but laughed about it, saying that would be like asking peanut butter to stay away from jelly.

I sighed loudly because I knew my upcoming confession would please her. "I saw him race through town with his lights flashing and I followed. So yes, we spoke."

Nana rolled her lips in to tamp down the grin she'd been wearing. "Was it murder? That's what people are saying."

"We'll have to wait for official word on that." I got up reluctantly from the comfy chair. A nice, long nap in my old nest sounded inviting, but I had places to go. I was sure Amy closed early on Sundays like me. "I just dropped by for a quick bite, then I have a few—a—a few errands to run."

"By the way, Hannah invited me over for some of her chili and cornbread tonight," Nana said.

"Of course, you're invited too. Unless you have something better planned." Hannah added in that same coy smile.

"I do have plans,' I said. Both women clutched their cups and saucers and sat up with interest.

"Oh?" Nana asked.

"I'm having dinner at Cade's."

There was some collapse of jaunty postures, mostly Hannah's. She was particularly invested in me ending up with Dalton. Nana had more of an insider's view, and as much as she dreamt of me ending up with my lifelong crush, she was also very fond of Cade.

"Not sure if the two of you heard this or not through the big rumor mill, but Dalton Braddock is getting married this June… and it's not to me."

Nana clucked her tongue. It was her signal to remind me to stop being a smart aleck. I'd heard that tongue click many times during my teens. Not so much in my forties.

Hannah sipped her tea and smiled. "We'll see."

I toasted some bread, smeared it with peanut butter and downed both pieces with a cold milk chaser. Hannah and

Nana bundled up for a walk in the neighborhood. I waved to them as I drove off.

Amy Dency was dusting some vintage glassware in the front window as I walked past. A few people were looking at a Victorian era settee, complete with intricately carved cherry wood arms and legs. Otherwise, the store was empty.

"Hello, Scottie," Amy said as she stepped down from the window display. "Are you back for those bookshelves?"

"No, I wasn't looking for shelves. That was Cade, and he's going a different direction."

Amy frowned. "I should have inspected all that junk Henry sold me much closer. Much closer," she muttered to herself. I was sure that had to do with the penny. It was true that Amy dealt in antiques, and she was an expert when it came to labeling something Victorian or Edwardian, but I doubted she had the same expertise when it came to coins. They were in a collector's category all by themselves. She would have seen the penny and shut the cigar box without giving it another thought… like most of us.

I decided to wait and see if Amy brought up the murder. Her store was a few miles away from Ripple Creek, so it was possible the news of Rusty's death hadn't reached her yet.

"I've got some beautiful, old apothecary jars in the back. They'd look great in your vintage-themed bakery."

"I'll give them a look." It seemed I'd been right. Amy wasn't aware of the murder. "What's happening with that penny?" I asked. Sometimes, in these investigations, I had no choice but to be the spark starter.

Her mouth pulled tight as she shoved her dust rag into

her back pocket. "Rusty won't answer any calls. He's avoiding everyone, it seems."

"Have you gone to see him? Have you been by his house?" I asked.

"I don't even know where he lives." Her eyes widened. "Do you? Maybe I should go see him after I close the shop. I can talk to him calmly, rationally, and explain to him why the coin is half mine. I mean a million dollars is a lot of money, and Rusty is pretty old. He doesn't have that much longer to spend it." Less time than she realized.

"I'm not sure that would be the kindest way to approach your argument for the penny. You know—I was coming home late last night from a friend's house (all a smooth lie) and I thought I saw you taking a walk. (More lies but sometimes they were necessary.) Do you have a big gray dog?"

"No, I'm a cat person." She nodded toward her cat. He was curled up on the counter near the register. "I'd never walk alone that late. There are too many critters out there, not to mention the possibility of weirdos lurking in the shadows. I have the same routine every Saturday night. I close the shop, heat up a can of soup, take a long bubble bath and then I sit in bed and read novels until I doze off. It's funny how when you're twenty all you can think about is going out to dance and meet friends. And then the forties creep up on you and the things that really get your motor purring are long baths and book reading in bed."

"Can't argue with that." As badly as Amy wanted that fancy car and her share of the fortune, she wasn't giving off murderer vibes. She lived alone, so no one could vouch for her whereabouts, but her alibi sounded plausible and genuine. Of course, if she'd killed Rusty, she might have worked on that story so she had an alibi ready to go. She'd recited her Saturday night routine voluntarily. Was it an act?

Amy glanced over at the couple looking at the settee. "Those apothecary jars are in the back of the store," she said and headed their direction.

"Right." I walked over to pet her cat. He was curled up on top of the Mercedes brochure. She was still thinking about that dream car. That was when I noticed a pile of old pennies sitting in a vintage ashtray. I moved a few around casually to check the dates.

"Are you interested in the ashtray?" Amy asked rather sharply from behind. She seemed to be upset that I was looking through the coins.

"No, I just noticed you had a lot of old pennies."

"They came out of the register. I decided if that one penny could be worth so much money, then maybe I had another valuable one just sitting in the register waiting to be discovered."

"I see. I guess we should all check our old coins."

Her face looked sterner. "That's right. Well, if you'd like, I could show you the glassware."

"No, another time. I just remembered I need to be somewhere. See you later."

Amy crossed her arms angrily as she watched me leave the shop. My visit had started pleasantly enough, but it went south after she caught me looking through her pennies at the counter. Maybe she wasn't so innocent after all.

twenty-four
. . .

I DROVE BACK to town and happened to spot Daniel and Cameron walking into the coffee shop. It was late enough in the afternoon that the shop was mostly empty. I planned to catch up to them, but a call from Dalton delayed that.

I answered. "For two people who are supposed to be staying away from each other, we are certainly spending a lot of time talking."

"What can I say," he chuckled. "There aren't that many people worth chatting with in this town, so you're my default friend."

"I'm trying to decide if that's good or bad. What did the coroner say?"

"Murder. He can't say anything definite until the post-mortem, but, as we suspected, Rusty died from a blow to the head. Coroner confirmed, due to the size and shape of the wound, that it could have been made by the wrench. I sent the wrench to forensics for fingerprints. So here I stand—or sit. I'm in my truck with a notepad that has few details and few possible suspects. Sally told me about the barking dog at just past midnight. I also had to hear a rundown of all the times a bear has lumbered through the neighborhood to wreak havoc. She also managed to keep me an extra twenty minutes by showing me family photos. I didn't realize she had three kids. They live all over the United States. Maybe some of them should stop by occasionally. Sally is lonely, and she's fretting about not having Rusty as a neighbor. They hung out, apparently."

"That's what she told me too. I don't think she's a suspect, do you?"

"She knew very little about the coin except that Rusty told her he might have found a rare one. She admitted that she tuned out whenever Rusty started talking about his coins. She said she had no interest in his collection. She tried to learn about them and even took out a few books from the library so they could chat about his coins occasionally, but she just couldn't work up any enthusiasm."

"Wow, you really had a nice, long visit." I glanced toward the coffee shop. It seemed the men were staying in with their coffees. Daniel sat down on the window side of a table.

"She made coffee and pulled out her favorite pack of caramel crème cookies. I knew they were her favorite because she talked about the first time she tried them. Her late husband brought them along on a date at the drive-in theater. And let me just add that drive-ins were a thing from the past that should have stayed relevant."

"I agree. Then if your notebook is empty, you'll be needing some names," I said.

"Yes, please, please, please."

"Well, if you're going to beg, I'll give you a few. There is the obvious—Cameron Burke. Apparently, Cameron and Rusty had a very competitive friendship and not just at the chess tables. Cameron was not terribly happy about the prospect that Rusty found a rare, valuable coin. He was jealous, and after Daniel determined it was a fake, Cameron was quite gleeful."

"Nice friend."

"Yep. Then there's Amy Dency."

I could hear his pen scraping across the paper. "You mean the woman who owns the antique shop on the highway?"

"The very same. I was in the antique shop with—" I stopped. It was silly, but I knew all I had to do was bring up Cade's name and I'd hear Dalton's teeth clench through the phone. "I was in the shop, and Rusty was there browsing through the store. I noticed his whole demeanor changed once he opened an old cigar box. He hurried to buy the box and left the store. The penny was in that box. Now Amy is claiming she should get half the money. She wants to buy a Mercedes."

"So, she wants half the money from a coin that is worthless? Not sure that'll be enough for a Mercedes."

"And that brings me to the second layer of the finders-keepers cake. Henry Voight had sold Amy that cigar box along with a lot of old stuff from his basement just a few hours earlier. Henry thinks he should get half the money."

"Half of the worthless coin," Dalton repeated.

"Exactly."

"How on earth do you get all these details?"

"You'd be surprised what goes on in a local bakery. It's far more than bread baking and cake decorating. Anyhow, I've got one of the suspects cornered in the coffee shop."

"What? No, don't do anything dangerous," Dalton said. "Remember the crazy photographer."

"How could I forget? And I guess *cornered* was the wrong choice of word. Cameron is sitting inside the coffee shop with Daniel Lomax, the appraiser. I thought I'd have a casual chat with them."

"See, that's where you have the advantage. My shiny badge is more of a hinderance than a help. Everyone gets defensive and clams up when I try to have a *chat*. I'll let you go. Let me know if you hear anything interesting."

"I certainly will. Bye." I hung up and couldn't keep from smiling. Dalton Braddock needed me for a case. My inner twelve-year-old was as positively giddy about that as when she learned he'd wanted to ask me to the spring dance.

I walked in and headed straight to the counter. I didn't want the men to think I'd followed them in. I ordered a hot tea and glanced casually around at the mostly empty coffee shop. Cameron's back was facing me. The way he was hunched over his coffee made me think he knew about Rusty. Daniel seemed to be comforting him, talking to him softly and even occasionally reaching across to pat Cameron's arm. Daniel looked up for a second, recognized me and waved.

I took that as my cue. I got my tea and walked over to

their table. "Hello." I looked at Cameron. His eyes were teary, and his face was blotchy. "I heard." I pointed at the empty chair.

Daniel invited me to sit. I sat down and put my hand on Cameron's shoulder. "Just terrible news."

Cameron nodded shakily. "Who would do something like this? Rusty was a good guy." He lifted a napkin and wiped his nose. "I'm simply beside myself. I'm just lucky to have my dear friend, Daniel, here to help me through this. He's even offered to stay one more day. Really, Dan, it's too much to ask. You have all those appointments in the city tomorrow. I'll manage."

Daniel shook his head. "Nonsense. I can move the appointments."

"Did either of you talk to or see Rusty last night?" I asked.

Cameron unfolded the napkin and refolded it, then used the clean side to wipe his nose again. "Daniel and I stayed up late watching movies. We were late for chess this morning because we overslept. Boy, I sleep like a rock when I've had a couple of beers."

"You should have a few tonight," Daniel suggested. "Something tells me you'll have a hard time sleeping."

"Good idea." Cameron looked down at the cup in front of him. "I guess I shouldn't be drinking coffee so late in the afternoon, but it was the only thing that sounded good." He patted his stomach. "Can't even think about food today." Cameron lowered his face and rubbed his forehead. "Who could have done this?"

"I was hoping you might have some idea," I said. Daniel

looked baffled by my statement. "I'm in contact with Ranger Braddock," I explained. "He's gathering evidence and talking to witnesses as we speak." I returned my attention to Cameron. "Was Rusty having trouble with anyone in the coin club or at the chess table? Did the rest of the club hear that the penny was a fake?"

Cameron took a steadying breath. "I was getting inundated with texts and emails from the other club members asking whether the penny was real or not. I tried to call Rusty this morning to ask if I could let them know, but there was no answer." His shoulders drooped. "I guess I know why. At the time I thought he was just being stubborn. I sent a group text to the club members to let them know that the penny was a fake. There was no reason for any of them to think differently. I'll tell you who I think killed Rusty."

Daniel looked at him disapprovingly.

"Dan, I know you told me not to start throwing out accusations, but Henry Voight was sure that coin was real. He told Rusty he was prepared to get a lawyer to fight for possession of the penny." Cameron chuckled sadly. "Can you imagine hiring an expensive lawyer to fight for a piece of metal that was worth a cent? Ranger Braddock should be talking to Henry Voight, and I'll tell him so when I see him."

Was Cameron looking to cast the blame somewhere else? He seemed genuinely distraught, but maybe he was upset because he knew he'd killed his old friend, Rusty.

"Well, Cameron, I think we should get you home. I'll make you a sandwich. You haven't eaten all day," Daniel said.

"Don't know what I'd do without you, Dan. I think I might

be able to eat a small sandwich." Cameron looked at me. "You tell Ranger Braddock I need to see him. We need to find who did this and fast. My poor, poor friend. I can't believe he's gone." His voice wavered, and his hands were shaky as he stood up from the table.

"Don't worry, Cameron. Ranger Braddock will catch the killer. I'm sure you'll be hearing from him soon."

twenty-five

. . .

I'D SPOKEN to Amy and Cameron. I had one more stop to make on my investigation. Henry Voight's house was only a short distance from Rusty's. It was a mid-century brick home with small windows and some old pines shading the front yard. The door to his garage was open. His old Chevy truck was parked in the driveway. A small sedan was parked in the garage. I walked up the driveway and noticed that Henry had his tools hanging on the side wall of the garage. They were neatly organized. I circled around the old truck and stepped inside the garage. The tools were arranged by size. Most of them had the Exeter brand name on the handles. I didn't see a large wrench. Was it possible I'd already found the killer?

"I thought I saw you walk up," Henry said.

I spun around. "Henry, hello." I was slightly breathless from being caught by surprise and the possibility that I was standing in front of a murderer. "Uh, I came to see you, but I was drawn into the garage by your wonderfully organized wall of tools. I've heard the Exeter brand is the best."

"Only kind I buy." His tone had become more congenial. "I like to keep my tools in order. That way I'm not looking around in some cluttered toolbox for a hammer or wrench." As he said it, his focus was pulled to the wall. His chin dropped. "Oh no, my wrench is gone." I followed him. There were empty nails between some pliers and a level. Henry rubbed his temple. "I'm sure I put it back after I used it. I had a leaky faucet in the service porch. No, I definitely put it back. I remember because Arlene had parked her car too close to the wall, and I had to scoot past it to get to the tools. We had an argument about it. In fact, that argument included me telling her that she had to stop leaving the garage door open. And now look what's happened. My Exeter wrench is gone."

"But would a thief come up here and take just the one piece?"

"It does seem strange, doesn't it?" Henry shook his head. "Must have been last night. After midnight, I heard a noise outside. I let it go at first. Lots of bear activity right now." Those darn bears were sure getting in the way of things for this case. "I finished the show I was watching and then got up to make sure the lid on my trash can was secure. Nothing messier than a hungry bear. I stepped out and noticed that, once again, Arlene had left the garage open. I shut it, checked the trash and then went inside to tell Arlene she'd forgotten the door again. I never thought to check if all the tools were there."

His story seemed true and unrehearsed but then he'd had time to come up with it. Henry moved closer to the wall and touched the two empty nails as if that might bring back his wrench. Had it been stolen, or was he having regrets about killing Rusty with it?

"Henry, have you heard the news about Rusty?"

He finally pulled his attention away from the wall. "Then it's true? Rusty is dead? Arlene heard about it from her friend, Pam, but I assumed it was just a rumor. What happened?"

"Not sure if there's official word on that. Have you spoken to Rusty lately? I know you were hoping to get half the money from the rare coin."

His thick brows bunched. "You mean the worthless penny?"

"I'm surprised to hear you say that. I spoke to Rusty yesterday, and he told me you'd shown up at his house threatening legal action for your half of the money. He said you didn't believe that the penny was worthless."

Henry's face dropped, and he stuck his hands in his pockets. It was a much more defeated posture than when I saw him at the park. "I did some research on those 1943 Lincoln copper pennies since then, and it seems most are fakes. People even take copper pennies from a different year and use tools to change the date. I was so excited about the possibility that it was real and that I might get a large sum of money that I let my emotions get away from me. This whole thing got blown out of proportion and all over a worthless coin." It seemed to suddenly occur to him that Rusty's death was connected to the penny. His face shot up. "Did someone kill Rusty? Pam mentioned that, but again, I figured that was just Pam with one of her wild rumors. Gossip is her drug of choice. I'm always telling Arlene to take everything Pam says with a good dose of skepticism. My gosh, did someone kill Rusty over that darn penny?"

"There's been no official word yet," I repeated. I was trying to decide whether to be impressed that Henry figured it out so easily or worried that he hadn't needed to figure it out at all because he knew exactly what happened. "You might get a visit from Ranger Braddock."

"Really?" he asked. "Why would he come here? I certainly had nothing to do with Rusty's death. Does he think I had something to do with it? Sure, I had words with Rusty about that stupid coin—" He rubbed his forehead. "I wish I'd never cleaned out that darn basement. That junk had been sitting there for years, and now look at the trouble it's caused."

The front door opened, and Arlene stepped out. She was wearing a pink and white striped sweater, and she hastily tossed a scarf around her neck. "I was wondering who you were talking to out here, Henry." Arlene smiled at me. "Good to see you, Scottie." She looked puzzled about why the town baker would be standing on the driveway talking to her husband.

Some of the puzzlement rubbed off on Henry. "Why did you come to see me?" Henry asked. His tone was less friendly. "I assume it wasn't for advice on how to organize your tools." He waved at the wall. Fortunately, his mention of tools reminded him about the garage door. He looked at

Arlene. "I've told you again and again not to leave the garage door open. Someone stole my wrench."

Arlene couldn't stop a laugh. "You mean to tell me someone walked into the garage and plucked one tool off the wall before making a clean getaway?"

"Well, look at that wall. The wrench is gone."

Arlene chuckled again. The turn in conversation had gotten me out of having to explain my visit. "You used it to fix the sink in the service porch. You probably left it there. I'll go get it, then you can hang it up on your precious tool wall. You're forgetful these days."

"I left the television on *one* time," he called to her as she headed into the house to find the wrench.

Henry was flustered enough by the conversation with Arlene that he seemed to have forgotten his last question. I didn't want to leave before finding out the ending to the wrench story, so I made something up. "I came by to ask you about those old bookshelves in Amy's store. Do you know their history? I have a friend who loves antiques and needs bookshelves."

Henry blew out a puff of breath. "Not that old junk again," he muttered. "Look, the old owner left that stuff down in the basement. I don't know anything about any of it. But if you ask me—I'd stay away from all of it. Those bookshelves weren't sturdy. They'll need a lot of repairs."

Arlene came back out of the house. She wasn't holding a wrench as she shook her head. "Guess you must have left it somewhere else," she said.

"I sure did," Henry said sharply. "It was right there on two empty nails. But since you can't be bothered to shut the garage door, someone else is using my expensive Exeter wrench."

"I'll see you both later," I said. I'd left behind a reasonable excuse for the visit.

Henry insisted he'd put aside his dreams of getting rich off a penny. Was he just saying that to erase any possible motive he had for killing Rusty? And then there was the matter of the murder weapon. Clearly, the Exeter wrench sitting in the forensics lab belonged to Henry Voight. Fingerprints would prove that. But why the sloppy cover-up? If Henry knew the wrench could be traced back to him, would he have tossed it in the trash? Or was someone trying to frame Henry?

All the questions were giving me a pinch of a headache. I'd had enough investigating for one afternoon.

twenty-six

. . .

"IT'S A CHILLY SPRING NIGHT, but the sky is clear and the stars are glittering like diamonds." Cade turned away from the window with his glass of wine. "Want to bundle up and take a walk around the garden?"

"Sure." I put down my glass of wine, got up from the couch and plucked my coat off the back of the settee. We'd ordered pizza and had a nice dinner filled with laughter and good conversation, two things that were never lacking when I was with Cade. I told him about Rusty's murder and my day of investigation.

We were both sufficiently layered for the brisk night air. Cade had done a lot of work, both hired and DIY, in the vast gardens around his home. It had been an overgrown, out-of-control landscape when he moved in. The planter beds were tangled with weeds and thick grass, and the stone steps leading from one garden to the next were cracked and hazardous to walk on. New pavers created an attractive, easy-to-meander pathway from the top garden to the bottom. New rosebushes waited to show off their blooms once the weather improved. The tender green buds from impending tulips and daffodils were just starting to break through the soil.

Cade and I walked along the path. "This garden is going to be beautiful," I said.

"I noticed the bulbs are starting to grow. I planted enough tulips to make Holland green with envy."

"They'll be spectacular, I'm sure. Spring is always a little behind up here, but when it does arrive, it delivers a full explosion of color."

We stopped at the bottom of the garden where a nice splash of moonlight was bathing the surrounding landscape in light. "It's so quiet out here," I said. "I mean it's not exactly Grand Central on Nana's street, but there are far more lights and neighbor noises."

"I decided to keep the place, rather than sell it, for exactly that reason. It was supposed to help me become a better, more productive writer."

"Except that you are a far better and more productive procrastinator."

Cade chuckled. It was a deep, rich sound that I loved. He put his arm around my shoulder. "Not my fault. There is just too much to entertain me around here. And then there is the matter of a very entertaining and likable baker in the area. I can't seem to get enough of her baked goods and her company."

I turned slightly in his arms. "I enjoy your company, too, Cade."

And then it happened. So many times, I'd imagined it was about to take place. We'd come so close so often, but this time he didn't hesitate. Cade's arms went around me, and he lowered his mouth to mine. It was a gentle, tentative kiss from both sides. We parted and I stared up at him. His hazel gaze looked almost silver in the moonlight.

"I'm not entirely sure why I did that," he started. "I suppose it's because I've wanted to kiss you since we first met. I don't blame you if you now turn around and walk away. I've ruined our friendship, haven't I? I'm a one-man demolition crew. I just risked everything on a kiss, and if I'm being honest, it wasn't really one of my better kisses. I'm out of practice and feeling far less confident than I usually feel when I make the move to kiss a—"

I pressed my finger against his mouth.

He stared down at me. "I'll shut up now," he mumbled past my finger.

I lowered my hand. My feelings about the kiss were so jumbled, I was at a loss for words. I'd been wanting it, and I was not disappointed. But like Cade, I worried about losing what we had together—a fun, no-strings-attached friendship. The kiss had turned this into something more. "Maybe we should—erase the last few minutes, so we can take time to think this through."

Cade nodded in disappointment. "You're right. I said I wasn't going to start this because you're still in love with Braddock."

"I'm not," I said. "Dalton is getting married. Sometimes I think you've created that whole scenario as an excuse not to move this further."

Cade stepped back and laughed dryly. "Trust me, Ramone, that is not the case. I've been wanting to move ahead for months, but I kept telling myself, 'Don't be a sap, Rafferty, you're second fiddle in all this. If you make a move, you'll lose her entirely, and that's the last thing you want.'"

I lifted a brow. "You literally had that conversation with yourself?"

"In third person and everything."

We both stared at each other for a second, then smiles broke out.

"You know what? I've been a fool," Cade said. He pulled me into his arms and kissed me again, a proper kiss, a yep-that's-the-one-I-was-waiting-for kiss.

When I finally stepped out of his embrace, my head was spinning and my knees were wobbly. Cade opened his mouth to say something. I held up my hand to stop him. "Let's end the evening on that terrific kiss and not one of your lengthy speeches about how you shouldn't have done it."

Cade nodded.

"I'm going to head home because it's been a long day what with people buying muffins and getting murdered and all that." I pointed clumsily in the wrong direction.

Cade pointed out the right way to the car.

"Right. Car is down there. I'm a little discombobulated because of that whole kiss thing," I said.

Cade smiled and put out his arm for me to take. We

walked to the house so I could get my things and then he walked me to the car. "Never mind, the silent Cade mode is kind of freaking me out."

"Thank goodness. Are you sure you don't want to stay for another glass of wine?" he asked. "I promise to be on my best behavior."

I patted his chest and smiled up at him. "I had a wonderful evening, Mr. Rafferty."

"Me, too, Ramone."

I was glad the drive home was short. I was still replaying the kiss in my head when I pulled up to Nana's house. Headlights flashed off my rearview mirror temporarily blinding me. The vehicle pulled in front of me and parked. It was Dalton's truck. The way he'd driven up made me think something else had happened.

I got out of the car as he was stepping out of his truck. "Dalton? What's wrong?"

His expression was unreadable as he walked toward me.

"Did someone else get murdered?" I asked.

"No, although I might be the next victim," he quipped.

"What? Why would you be next?" My mind had gone directly to Rusty's murder, but he had something entirely different on his mind.

"I broke up with Crystal," he blurted. "It's over. Her parents will probably send a hitman or, at the very least, their lawyers after me, but I had to end it."

I was taking it all in slowly because I'd already had a somewhat destabilizing night. "Are you sure about this? Maybe it's just jitters."

He shook his head as I spoke. "Not the jitters. We aren't suited for each other, and there's no way we could make each other happy. Besides that, I can't marry Crystal Miramont because I'm in love with someone else."

I hadn't expected the last part, and admittedly, it was a little disappointing to hear. "You are?"

Dalton moved closer and smiled down at me. "It's the same girl I've been in love with since grade school. She's smart, beautiful, generous and she bakes an amazing cheese Danish."

I was speechless. Was this real or maybe I'd dreamt this whole night?

"Dalton, I don't know what to say."

"You don't have to say anything right now. I just needed to tell you." He leaned forward and kissed my forehead, then got back in his truck.

I wandered up to the door in a cloud. The dizziness left behind by both kisses had morphed into a kind of brain fog. I looked back to watch Dalton's truck pull away. I think I now understood that old saying, "when it rains, it pours."

I walked inside. Nana had fallen asleep on the couch. I picked up the throw blanket and tucked it in around her. She stirred and then opened her eyes. "Scottie, you're home. How was your night?"

"Let's just say—different than any I've ever experienced. I'll fill you in in the morning. Goodnight, Nana."

"Goodnight, Button."

twenty-seven

...

USUALLY ON MY DAY OFF, I'd wake to the smell of pancakes and bacon, but not this morning. I was disappointed because I needed a pancake chat with Nana more than anything. I'd slept solidly, considering the turmoil going on in my head. Nana left a note in front of the coffee pot.

"Regina and I are going to breakfast at the diner down the hill. See you soon. Can't wait to hear about your evening."

My phone beeped. It was still on my nightstand. Was it Cade? Had he written a long message about why he shouldn't have gone through with the kiss? Had any kiss ever come with so much baggage? I doubted it. Maybe it was Dalton telling me he'd temporarily lost his mind and that he'd patched things up with Crystal. I was sure both men had woken with big heaps of regret. I picked up my phone and was relieved. The text was from Esme.

"Want to meet for some coffee?"

"Yes. A half-hour?" I texted back.

"See you at the coffee shop."

I desperately needed to talk to my friend about my night. I needed advice from an outsider because my head was too muddled to make sense of any of it. I showered, got dressed and drove to town. I practically ran when I saw Esme walking up from her car.

"I'm in desperate need of a therapy session, because I might be going crazy," I said.

"Oh, wow. Sounds like you had a way better afternoon off than me. I settled onto my couch with a book, and Earl promptly crawled into my lap and coughed up a hairball on my chest. Then Salem refused to eat her food, and I tripped over Trina and landed on my knees."

"Oh my gosh, you poor thing," I said. We stepped inside the coffee shop. It was a quiet Monday morning. Most of the commuters had already been in for their morning cups.

We bought our coffees and sat down at one of the tables. "How are your knees?" I asked.

"Sore. That's the hazard of having a deaf cat. Earl and Salem are good about moving out of the way, but poor Trina doesn't always see me coming." She took a sip of her coffee with closed eyes. "Hmm, that's the stuff. I was out of coffee at home."

"Nana went to breakfast at the diner. She usually makes pancakes when I'm off. And don't I sound like a spoiled little kid?"

"Those are the perks of living with a wonderful grandmother." She took another sip of coffee. "Now tell me all about it. What happened last night?" She put up her hand. "Wait, I can see it in that blush on your face. Cade kissed you."

"Way to ruin a girl's explosive news," I said.

Esme laughed. "You're right. Bad friend, Esme. Forget I just said that, and let's start from the top. What happened last night?"

I raised a brow. "Cade kissed me," I said plainly.

"I knew it. How was it?"

I sipped my coffee in thought. *How was it?* "It was good and awkward and complicated. I was glad he did it. You know—finally ripped the bandage off and all that."

Esme sat back hard. "Was it that bad? I mean that analogy is usually used for something you want to get over with."

I sat up and thought about my words. Had I wanted that? Had I wanted to get the kiss over with? "I think I meant it was always hanging in the air around us, and now that it's happened, that tension is gone. I think we might be able to move forward with this now."

Esme laughed. "'Think' and 'might?' Not sure there are two more passive and less romantic words in the English language."

"It's not easy being best friends with a bookstore owner."

Esme smiled. "Are we best friends?"

Here I was again—moving mountains in my social life. "I'd like to think we are."

"Good, because I feel the same."

I sighed. "I'm glad. I'm feeling so off balance with everything that's happened."

Esme leaned forward. "Was there more than the kiss?"

Before I could answer, Cameron Burke came into the coffee shop. He looked distraught as he surveyed the room. He spotted me and walked straight over to our table.

"Cameron, are you all right?" I asked. I pointed to an empty chair, but he shook his head.

"I need to talk to you, Scottie. I've got something important to tell you."

"I could leave and let you speak to her alone," Esme said.

Cameron's hands were shaky as he pulled them free from his coat pockets. "No, I don't want to interrupt. And I don't want to talk here." He was certainly acting strangely. Was he planning to confess to Rusty's murder? "Can you stop by my house after you're through with coffee?"

"Absolutely, Cameron."

He nodded. "Thanks." He skittered out almost as quickly as he came in.

Esme and I watched him leave, then she turned to me. "What on earth was that about? Do you think it has to do with Rusty's death?"

"I think so."

"What if Cameron did it? Maybe you should call Dalton, so he can meet you at the house."

The second she mentioned Dalton, something new and bothersome occurred to me. What was going to happen when we met up again? Things were going to be awkward. He'd blurted out that he'd loved me since grammar school. Was that possible? Could the crush have been reciprocated? How on earth did I miss the cues? Although, in my defense, I was a kid and probably not terribly dialed in to the world of boys. I still wasn't… apparently.

"What are you not telling me?" Esme asked. "I said Dalton and you blushed and the blush was followed by a lost and starry-eyed look." She pointed at me. "It's still there."

I hesitated. What if I was right, and my earlier notion that Dalton would soon text and tell me he was just acting crazy last night and he'd gotten back together with Crystal came true? I'd die of embarrassment. I was also looking at a friend who wasn't going to leave the coffee shop without hearing the whole story. At the same time, I was anxious to talk to Cameron. Was he planning to confess? Did he find out something that would help lead to the killer? And where was his friend, Daniel? I thought he'd planned to stay another day to help Cameron through his shock and grief.

"You are delaying, my friend." Esme said. "Which leads me to believe that you have some big news. Shall I guess it?"

I shrugged teasingly. "Go ahead and try. I guarantee you won't have seen this one coming, because I certainly didn't." I casually picked up my coffee and took a sip.

"Dalton broke up with Crystal," Esme said.

I covered my mouth to avoid spitting out the coffee. It took me a second to stop coughing.

"Aha, I'm right," she said.

"You're positively psychic. How could you possibly have guessed that?"

She lifted her eyes coyly. "I confess I didn't pull this out of thin air or from the starry-eyed look sitting across from me. I stopped at Roxi's market to buy some coffee before I came here. Dalton was at the refrigerator section picking out a sandwich and his phone rang. He let it ring several times, then finally answered it. I could tell he was talking to Crystal, and he was trying to calm her down. He said something about how it 'never would have worked.'"

I actually felt sorry for Crystal, which was not easy to do. "He stopped by the house last night."

"After the Cade kiss?" Esme asked.

I nodded. "I felt like I got hit by two torpedoes both coming from opposite directions." I decided to leave off the part about him declaring that he loved me. He wasn't thinking straight because he'd just broken up with Crystal. I was sure he'd rethink that proclamation again.

Esme was too smart though. "He came to tell you because he loves you."

I didn't confirm or deny.

"What are you going to do?" Esme asked.

I sighed as I spun the coffee cup between my hands. I looked up at her. "Move to a new town?"

She laughed. "Two hunky men both interested in you. You *poor* thing," she said with an eyeroll. "And you can't move to a new town because you're my best friend."

"What *am* I going to do?" I asked.

Esme lifted her cup. "Don't know, but I'm going to have to pop some popcorn because I think I'm in for a good show."

"Not helpful, best friend."

twenty-eight
...

NANA RARELY USED THE PHONE. She'd only started using a cell phone a few years back after my insistence. Her house didn't have great cell phone reception, so she avoided making calls. Whenever she did call, it worried me. "Nana, is everything all right?"

"Of course, it is. Regina is driving us back from the diner. I'm sorry I wasn't there to make pancakes and hear about your night." I could hear Regina asking questions in the background.

Nana didn't pull the phone away when she addressed Regina. "I'm talking to her now. Give me a second and I'll ask." A small, exasperated puff of air came through the phone. "Are you home? We can sit down for a nice chat when I get back."

"Actually, I'm heading to Cameron Burke's house. He said he had something to tell me."

"Did Cameron kill Rusty?" Regina asked loudly.

"I imagine you heard that since she's using her megaphone voice," Nana quipped.

"I don't know who killed Rusty," I said. "She'll have to wait until Dalton makes an arrest. I'm just getting to Cameron's cabin. I'll see you when I get home." I parked in front of Cameron's house. It was an old cabin not far from Henry's place. The front porch seemed to be leaning a little to the left and multi-paned windows were trimmed in bright green. Cameron's car was in the driveway. His was the only car parked in front of the cabin.

I walked up to the front door and knocked. There was no answer. I knocked again. I leaned closer to the door. "Cameron, it's me, Scottie." I stood there a few more minutes, then walked around to the front window. The panes were dusty from the long winter. I rubbed a hole in the dirt and peered through. A light was on in the kitchen, but I couldn't see anything else. I knocked on the window just to be sure. Still no response.

I walked around to the backyard, went through the small gate and stepped onto the back patio. I glanced through the sliding door and gasped. The back door let me see into the kitchen. Cameron was on the floor. I pounded on the glass door. "Cameron!" He didn't stir.

I pulled out my phone and called Dalton. He answered on the first ring. "Scottie, I—uh—I guess we should talk." There it was—his regret and apology tour waiting to begin. But there was no time for that now. He'd have to "let me down easy" later.

"Dalton, I'm standing outside Cameron Burke's house. He asked me to drop by, but he wasn't answering the door. I can see him on the floor, and he's not moving."

"I'll call for an ambulance," Dalton said. "I'm only five minutes out."

I kept knocking on the glass door hoping to see some movement inside but to no avail. Dalton made good on his word. His truck pulled up five minutes later.

I met him out front. "I've been knocking, but he's not moving."

Dalton pounded on the door once and then stepped back and kicked it in. It splintered around the lock and flew open. Dalton rushed in first. I followed.

"Cameron," Dalton said urgently as he crouched down next to him. Cameron was on his side. Dalton placed his hand on Cameron's arm, and his expression turned grim. He lifted Cameron's limp hand and searched for a pulse. After a minute, Dalton looked up at me. "He's dead." He leaned closer to Cameron. "Looks like he has red marks around his neck."

"Strangled?" I asked. I finally took the time to glance around. The house was in disarray. Not as badly ransacked as Rusty's but someone was clearly looking for something. There was a glass of milk spilled on the counter and another glass broken on the floor near Cameron's head.

"Looks like he tried to fight off his attacker," Dalton said. "When I visited him yesterday, he had a friend with him."

"Daniel Lomax. He was the coin appraiser."

"Right, that's what he told me. They were each other's alibi for the night Rusty was killed. They'd been watching movies, then they went to bed. Cameron admitted he'd had more beers than usual and fell asleep like a rock."

"I saw Daniel with Cameron at the coffee shop yesterday. He told me he was staying an extra day to help Cameron through the shock of losing his friend Rusty. He never said how long he'd be staying today. I saw Cameron alive just an hour ago. I was in the coffee shop with Esme this morning when Cameron came in looking agitated. He was even a little shaky. Daniel wasn't with him. He told me he needed to talk to me, but he wanted to do it somewhere private so he told me to meet him at his house after my coffee."

"Did he give you any idea what it was about?" Dalton asked.

"No, but I assumed it had to do with Rusty."

"I have Daniel's number. I'll give him a call." The sirens were screaming in the distance. "Another race up the hill just to be told they're not needed. I'm going to go out and meet them, stop them before they start unloading."

"I'll have a look around. Do you have--?"

Dalton smiled faintly as he pulled a pair of gloves from his pocket. "Maybe we need to get you your own supply."

I put them on. My fingers were swimming in the latex. "Preferably ones that fit."

The ambulance pulled up to the house as Dalton stepped outside. Kitchen drawers had been left open and food had been taken out of the pantry. Once again I was looking for evidence in a house that had been torn apart. I walked into the living room. Cameron's vinyl record collection was strewn across the rug. Pieces of wood, originally stored in a big wicker basket on the hearth, now littered the floor. Throw blankets were, well, *thrown* about the place. I moved a pile of magazines around with my foot but saw nothing. I took a step back and landed on something hard. It was the television remote.

I picked it up and set it on the coffee table. As I put it down the battery hatch opened and something fell out. It clinked onto the table. It was a penny. I picked up the penny and looked at it closely. The date was 1943. It was Rusty's unlucky penny. What was Cameron doing with it? Had he killed Rusty? But then who killed Cameron?

I heard the ambulance doors slam and it pulled away. Dalton was walking toward the house with the phone to his ear. He was calling the coroner. It seemed another one of our citizens had been murdered. His phone rang again as he reached the broken front door. He answered it brusquely. "I told you we can talk tonight. I'm working. I can't talk right now." He hung up and looked flustered as he stepped inside.

He realized that I'd overheard his conversation. "This is harder than I expected," he admitted.

"The wedding plans got pretty far," I reminded him.

"Somehow, I imagined Crystal would just get angry, maybe cry and scream for a night, then she'd be on social media trying to meet someone new, someone who fits better with her lifestyle and family. Her dad never liked me. My name wasn't Rothschild or Rockefeller."

"I didn't realize he felt that way. Even rich, entitled people like Crystal can get their hearts broken. I feel sorry for her. I don't think it would be easy to get over losing Dalton Braddock."

His brown gaze held mine for a second, but this wasn't the time or place to talk about relationships. I held out my gloved palm. The troublesome penny sat in the middle of it.

Dalton stared down at my hand. "Is that what I think it is?"

"I'm no expert, but it says 1943 and the wonderful Mr. Lincoln is front and center, and since it was hidden in the back of the remote—I'd say yes, this is *the* penny."

Dalton took a plastic evidence bag out of his pocket. I handed over the coin. He held it up to the sunlight coming through the small front window. "Well, 1943, you've caused more than a penny's worth of trouble this week."

"I'll say. More like a million bucks' worth of trouble."

twenty-nine
...

THE CORONER ARRIVED twenty minutes later. As they set up for their investigation, Dalton and I stepped out to the front yard. A few neighbors looked on with concern. "I'll have to go talk to them. Maybe someone saw or heard something," Dalton said as he took out his phone and notepad. "First, I'm going to call Mr. Lomax." He dialed the number. "Hello, is this Daniel Lomax?"

I could hear an answer, then a loud racket came through the phone. It was so loud Dalton flinched and pulled the phone away from his ear. He put it on speakerphone. "Is that a jackhammer?"

"Yes, I'm walking to my office in the city. There's some construction going on across the street. How can I help you?" he asked.

"Mr. Lomax, when was the last time you saw Cameron Burke?"

"Cam?" He sounded perplexed. "Well, I saw him this morning around seven. We ate bowls of cereal and said goodbye. I had appointments I needed to get to in the city, so I left early."

"I see. How did Mr. Burke seem? Was he nervous or concerned about anything?" Dalton asked.

"Gee, not really. I mean he's been out of sorts since the murder but not particularly nervous. Why do you ask? What's this about? Is Cameron all right?"

"I'm sorry to tell you that Mr. Burke is dead," Dalton said. He waited for a reaction. There was a long pause.

"Dead? That's impossible. We just ate breakfast together. What happened?"

"The coroner will confirm cause of death later today. Were you two close? How did you know each other?"

It took him a second to find his words. He seemed genuinely shocked. "We met at coin collecting conventions and meetings. We spoke every month or so, mostly about coins. We didn't have much else in common. The poor man. I hope this isn't about that penny. People can sometimes get worked up about these things."

"I'm sure," Dalton said. "Did you notice anyone around Cameron's house, any cars?" There was a pause as the jackhammer started up again.

"No, I left right after we ate, and the road was quiet. Are you telling me he was murdered? How awful. What is going on up there in that small town?"

"A penny found in an old cigar box… apparently. I may need to call you with more questions."

"Of course, anything you need."

"Thank you for your time." Dalton added something to his notepad. "Well, if he's in the city, then he couldn't have killed Cameron. Unless, of course, he's lying about the time."

"But I saw Cameron just over an hour ago. That wouldn't give Daniel enough time to kill Cameron and drive to the city. Have you spoken to Henry Voight?" I asked.

Dalton nodded. "Yes, and guess which brand of tools he uses?"

"Exeter and his wrench is missing. I visited him yesterday. I just never got a chance to tell you."

"His wife, Arlene, told me it was her fault the tool was missing. She also corroborated his alibi that they were both in all night. I'll have to go back and talk to them. I should get back inside. Thanks for your help." He looked at me. "I'm hoping we'll get a chance to talk. I imagine you were pretty stunned by what I said last night."

I nodded. "Stunned is a good word."

His phone rang again. He sighed and his shoulders slumped as he looked at the screen. "It's Crystal's mom. I don't know how I'm going to repay them for this wedding. They spent a fortune. I never wanted a big, elaborate wedding."

"Still, I think you'll be on the hook for it," I said. "I'm going to head home. You've got your hands and head full right now. The talk can wait until you've smoothed out all your problems first."

Dalton looked disappointed, but he nodded. I got in my car and drove home. Nana was in the front yard filling the birdbath. She was working hard at holding back a grin as I walked across the yard toward her.

She turned off the hose, and the grin broke free.

"You know," I said.

"I do."

"How? Wait, never mind. You had breakfast with Regina. How does that woman hear news so fast?"

"She does have a knack for it," Nana said.

"I suppose she even knew about the kiss," I blurted. I was feeling a little cheated.

Nana's chin dropped. "Dalton kissed you?"

"What? No. Not Dalton—"

"Cade kissed you?" Nana took my hand. "Let's go inside. I need to hear everything."

"Think you've already heard it," I said as I took dejected steps toward the porch. "And the way news travels in this town, I'm sure everyone already knows that Cameron Burke is dead."

Nana stopped with a gasp. "Cameron is dead?"

I smiled. "You mean Regina didn't know that?" I lifted my chin. "Well then, finally I have some noteworthy news to deliver. Of course, it's tragic news, but still, I beat Regina to the punch on this one."

We went inside and sat down at the kitchen table with cups of tea. "We'll get the unpleasantries out of the way first," Nana said. "What happened to Cameron?"

"Looks like foul play." I knew for certain it was, but it wasn't my place to say. "Dalton is there right now."

His name came up, and a new grin appeared, although

weaker and edged with concern. "How is he doing? I'm sure the Miramont family isn't going to make this easy for him. Just like the Rathbones didn't make it easy for you."

"Yes, but fortunately, I had the means to repay them for all the expenses. They weren't out any money. Unless Dalton has some secret fortune, how's he ever going to repay them? From the snippets I was hearing about that wedding, it was going to be a royal affair with no expenses spared."

"Lavish weddings are always a risk. Did Dalton tell you about the breakup? When did you see him?"

"He showed up here last night just as I got back from Cade's house."

Another smile. "He wanted you to be the first to know. Did he have anything else to say?"

"Well, since you can always tell when I'm lying, a skill that terrified me as a kid, I'll just say yes, there was more to the conversation."

Nana clapped once. "He admitted that he has feelings for you."

I sat back. "Why do I hang around people with a sixth sense? How did you know?"

Nana waved off my comment. "Please, the man has never tried to hide it. You don't think he comes here for my silly soup dinners and pancake breakfasts?"

"Uh, yeah, I do."

Another wave off. "How did you respond?"

"Well, I was in shock, so I wasn't exactly articulate. Besides that, I'd just gotten home from Cade's house—"

Nana squeaked in excitement. "That's right, the kiss. How

could I forget that? Why on earth didn't you wake me last night, Button? I needed to hear all this when it was still fresh in your mind."

"Trust me, it's still fresh. Raw might even be the word for the way I'm feeling. And in the meantime, all the elderly gentlemen in town are being killed off over a penny."

"That's just terrible," she said quickly. "How was it?"

"The murder? About as grisly as one might expect."

Nana tapped my hand. "Oh stop. You know perfectly well what I meant."

I shrugged. "It was a good kiss. I just didn't get a chance to really think about it because I was hit with a one-two punch from Dalton."

Nana sipped her tea. "Hannah is going to go bananas when I tell her."

"Nana, please don't tell anyone about Dalton admitting his feelings for me. He was still charged up from the adrenaline of breaking off his wedding. He'll probably rethink that."

"No, he won't," she said confidently. "Now the question is—what are you going to do?"

"About what?"

"If you're going to be flippant about it, Button—" She moved to stand up.

"All right. I'm sorry. It's my way of coping with a problem that I have no way to tackle. I think, first, I'm going to spend the day finding out who killed Rusty and Cameron. Then, if I'm feeling up to it—I'm going to let myself think about my social life."

"That's smart, Button. Take time to reflect on everything."
"I will. But for now—I'm off to talk to a few suspects."

thirty
. . .

NORMALLY, when there was a case and I was nosing in on it, I'd just pick up the phone and call Dalton to ask questions. This time I stared at the phone for a minute wondering if I should call him. It was silly, of course. We'd just spent the morning together at Cameron's house, but now it felt weird calling him. Just like the kiss had made it harder to call Cade. Great. Now everything was weird between all of us, and that wasn't even counting the fact that both men despised each other. My goodness, had Nana been right? Did they dislike each other because of me? I guess my first question should've been how I could've possibly considered that Nana was wrong about something.

    Before I could move my thumb across the screen to dial Dalton, a call came in. It was Cade. For a second, I considered letting it go to voicemail. I wasn't sure I wanted to talk about last night yet, and besides that, there'd been two murders in town, and I wanted to get to the bottom of them. Cade would be hurt if I let it go to voicemail. He was already worried about how the kiss would affect our relationship.

"Hello," I said.

"Ramone, I wasn't sure you'd answer. In fact, I almost hung up because I didn't have a voicemail message ready to go." I was relieved that he'd moved right on to witty dialogue instead of talk about the kiss.

"Do you usually prewrite and rehearse those?" I asked.

"Occasionally, when I don't want to sound like a complete Neanderthal. I walked to the market and tales of murder and mayhem were flying yet again. Cameron, the coin aficionado?"

"Yep. I found him dead on the floor of his kitchen."

He paused. "How is it that you always manage to stumble on dead bodies? I think I need to hire you as a research assistant for my novels, or, at the very least, a muse. Your life is a literal thriller."

"Not by choice."

Another pause, which was unusual for Cade. "I guess if you found a dead body you had to call Braddock."

"He is the ranger, so yes, I called him." This was where the whole thing was going to get sticky and annoying. I didn't want to be in the middle of a triangle, no matter how much I liked both men. I changed the topic. "What are you up to today?" I asked.

"Same thing I'm up to most days. I'm writing. I thought we could get together later. It feels like we left things a little frayed and unsettled yesterday."

"Not frayed but maybe unsettled. I'll see about tonight. I've got to go to the bakery and put together the bread starters for tomorrow's loaves. Never a day off in baking land."

"Author land, too. Scottie," he began. He rarely called me by my first name. "I hope I didn't blow it. I've never felt so uneasy about a kiss."

"You haven't blown it and stop feeling uneasy. I'm glad you kissed me. I promise, we'll talk soon."

"All right. Later, Ramone."

"Later." I hung up and was about to call Dalton. He rang first. I preempted anything he might have said that had to do with *us*. One of those conversations at a time was plenty.

"What did the coroner have to say?" I asked.

"It was murder by strangulation, but we already knew that. There were a few fibers on his neck that seemed to indicate the killer had on gloves or used some sort of fabric to choke Cameron. They're being tested. I was on my way to interview Henry, but I got called up the hill to a break-in at one of the stores at the resort. I shouldn't be too long. I just hope I can avoid the entire Miramont clan while I'm up there. Unfortunately, my truck is easy to spot. Which brings me to another piece of news."

"Gosh, no more dead bodies, please."

"No, but I might have preferred that. Crystal's dad called with a threat. He said he had ties to enough people in power that he could see to my demotion. He mentioned something about wanting to see me cleaning public toilets and picking up litter in the parks."

"He can't do that, can he?"

"I wouldn't put it past him. He does have a lot of clout and important friends up here on this mountain. How are you on bakery employees? I've been known to dabble in baking now and then."

I laughed. "Scooping cookies out of a tub of premade cookie dough does not count as baking."

"Darn. That was going to be the first thing on my resumé. Well, I've got to go. Hopefully, I'll make an arrest on this case before they strip me of my badge and hand me the public bathroom list."

"I'm sorry about that, Dalton. You're having it rough. I don't envy you in all this."

"I'm almost at the resort. No sign of snipers or unmarked cars, so I guess I can go in. See you later."

I hung up the phone and drove toward Henry's house. He was still on the top of my list because of the missing wrench. It wasn't much to go on, and he had a plausible excuse for why it was missing, but I was short on ideas. Henry's old truck wasn't in the driveway. I was about to turn away when I spotted Arlene out watering a newly planted flower garden.

I parked and got out. Arlene glanced back to see who was walking up the driveway. She turned off the hose. "Gosh, that's twice in the same weekend. If I didn't know any better, I'd say you had a crush on my husband." She punctuated her comment with a laugh, but it was somewhat forced.

"Actually, I did come here to see Henry. I wasn't sure if he'd heard that Cameron Burke died this morning."

"Angie, down the street, was telling me that as she walked her dog past. How tragic. What is happening in our wonderful town? Henry went to the hardware store to buy a replacement wrench for the one that was stolen." She looked pointedly at the shut garage door. "I guess I have to be more careful. He's pretty sore at me about leaving it open and losing his wrench. A man and his tools, eh?"

"Maybe he heard about Cameron while he was out and about this morning." I was taking a convoluted path to his alibi. I knew Arlene had already corroborated his whereabouts the night before, when Rusty was killed, but now it seemed he'd need a second alibi.

Arlene shrugged. "Not sure how he'd have heard. He watched that darn baseball game all morning. Angie came by just twenty minutes ago after Henry had left. But I suppose the news will be all over town by now. You know how fast it travels in Ripple Creek."

"I do. Henry was watching the game all morning?" I asked.

"Can't pull him away from his sports. I had to feed him breakfast at the coffee table. Has Ranger Braddock made an arrest yet?"

"Not yet. I'm sure it'll happen soon."

"Hope so. And I hope our garage thief gets caught soon, too. Henry talked to Irving across the street about his stolen tool. Irving said his dog was barking around midnight. He got up to see why the dog was barking. He saw a figure leaving our driveway. He had a hood pulled up over his head, and he was hunched over as if hiding something. We figured it was the wrench."

"Did Irving get a good look at the person?"

"I'm afraid not. It was dark, and the person was covered by a hood. I just don't understand why they took the *one* tool. I mean if you're going to commit a crime and risk the possibility of getting caught, then at least make it worth your while."

"Good point. Maybe the person had a job that only required a wrench."

She laughed. "I suppose so."

"Nice talking to you." I walked away.

"Hey, when are you going to make those apple muffins again? I love those."

"I'm glad. They'll be back in fall." I waved and headed to my car. It seemed Henry had not one but two alibis. Of course, Arlene could've just been covering for him.

A text came through from Dalton. "The lab called. They found clear prints on the wrench all belonging to the same person. I'm sure they'll be a match for Henry. I'm going to see him after I'm done here."

"If they do match, does that mean an arrest?" I asked.

"No, that won't be enough to go on. It's Henry's wrench. His prints should be on there. I was really hoping they'd find two different sets of prints."

"That makes sense. All good up there at the resort?"

"Other than a lot of dirty looks from everyone—all good."

It was time to see the other person who badly wanted half of that penny money. Amy didn't usually open her antique shop on Mondays, but with any luck, I'd find her there organizing or doing paperwork. My suspect list was short, and at this point, it was going nowhere fast.

thirty-one
. . .

I REACHED the small lot in front of Amy's antique shop. It seemed I wasn't in luck. There were no cars in the lot, and the store was dark. I got out to double check. I peered into the shop. It was empty. I knocked once on the door, but there was no answer.

Tires crunched gravel behind me. It was Dalton. He parked his truck. The butterflies did their thing for a second, then calmed back down. Was that a sign that my feelings for Dalton weren't as strong? I smiled at that notion.

That, in turn, caused Dalton to smile. "I hope you have a good, funny story because I'm going to need one." His smile faded fast, and a look that could only be described as despair took over his handsome face.

"Oh, dear, a run-in with Crystal?"

"Worse. Her father. He is very serious about getting me fired. He said he didn't trust me to be fair and impartial when it came to taking care of the problems at the resort. Maybe he has a point."

"That's ridiculous. He's questioning your integrity as a police officer. That's not right."

Dalton's posture showed how much weight he was carrying on his shoulders. "I think he has every right to question my integrity." He straightened and took a deep breath. "Anyhow, I'm still wearing the badge, so I've got a job to do." He glanced at the dark store. "I guess you're here to see the same person as me."

"Yes, but she's not in today."

"I've got her address. She lives a mile away. I don't know Amy too well, and since she lives alone—I'd like it if you came along."

"I won't say no to that. I'll follow in my car," I added quickly. I wasn't ready for a car ride together.

"Right. Let's go."

We drove up the hill and turned onto the small road leading to Amy's house. A car was in the driveway. An old wooden wagon filled with silk flowers sat under a maple tree. We walked up to the door and knocked. The curtains pushed aside, and Amy peered cautiously out. It took her a second to unlock the door. She seemed to be fumbling with the latch. When she finally got the door open, her clumsiness was explained. Her right hand was swaddled in layers of gauze.

"I'm glad it's you, Ranger Braddock. I've been very nervous since I heard the news, first about Rusty and then Cameron. I knew there was more to that penny than I was being told." She motioned inside with her left hand. As expected, her house was a treasure trove of antique furniture. A round-edged, glass-door curio cabinet caught my fancy. It was filled with vintage glassware.

"Looks like you've had an accident," Dalton said.

"Yes, and if I seem a little fuzzy, it's the pain pills. I only just woke up." She held up the bandaged hand. "I was moving a few things around in the shop, and the glass door on a cabinet shattered. My hand slipped through the shards. It took seven stitches."

"I'm sorry to hear that. When did it happen?" Dalton asked.

"Last night. I was just finishing up in the shop. My friend, Billie, drove me down to the emergency room." She seemed to be figuring out what the ranger's visit was about. "I've got the doctor's release order with the date and time if you need to see it. Look, I know I threatened Rusty with legal action, but I certainly didn't kill him. He told me the appraiser declared the coin a fake, but I think his death, and now Cameron's, shows that the appraiser was wrong. Does anyone know where the penny is right now? I'll bet the person who killed Rusty and Cameron has it."

Dalton didn't let on about the penny's whereabouts. It had already caused enough havoc.

"We're keeping an eye out for it."

"It's a shame Rusty died before he got a second opinion. Irwin Babbington lives just five miles south of Ripple Creek. He's a retired jeweler. He used to make—"

"Jewelry with old coins," I chimed in.

"That's right. He knows a lot about coins," Amy said.

"You're right. My grandmother was good friends with Irwin. They used to meet for coffee, but Irwin stopped driving. He still lives down there on his own?" I asked.

"Yes, he's doing well, even after losing his wife, Donna. I take antique jewelry down to him occasionally for an appraisal. He's just off Moss Road, south of the river bend. But I guess that doesn't matter if there is no penny to look at." Amy's face fell into a frown as she looked at the coffee table in her front room. The Mercedes brochure was on top of it. "I guess I'll have to find a rich husband, so I can have my dream car."

I tilted my head at her. "You live high up in the Rocky Mountains. Would that car be practical?"

Amy sighed. "Probably not, but when are things we dream about ever practical?"

"Good point."

"I'll need a photo of your hospital release. Then I can take you off my list," Dalton said.

"I knew I was a suspect." Amy disappeared down the hallway and returned with a paper. "I guess it's lucky I cut my hand. This should clear me." She handed over the release form. Dalton took a quick photo. "Thanks for your time. Take care of that hand."

We walked out of the house. Dalton's phone rang. A frustrated groan followed. He answered reluctantly. "I'm working," he said curtly. I could hear Crystal's voice coming through. She sounded close to hysterical.

"Just calm down. I can't understand you."

I kept walking toward my car. I didn't want to intrude on

the conversation. I couldn't help but feel badly for Crystal. I glanced back. Dalton's face was down. He looked anguished, and he was rubbing his forehead. I considered getting in the car and driving off, but I had a question to ask him.

His look of pain intensified as he hung up. He walked toward me. "I've got to go see her. She's—she's—taking it a lot harder than I expected."

"Really?" I asked. "In a few months' time, she was supposed to be walking down the aisle in her, no doubt, designer gown, toward the man she loved. She is obviously one of those women who dreamt about her wedding all her life, and that dream was shattered with one conversation." My words seemed to make him feel even worse—if that was possible. "I'm not trying to upset you, Dalton. I'm just saying—look at it from her shoes."

"But is she upset about having her wedding ruined or is she upset about losing me? I think it's the wedding. Crystal is beautiful and rich. It won't take her long to find someone else."

"Unless this has shattered her confidence. Maybe she won't trust anyone after this."

"Thanks for the pep talk," he said dryly.

"I'm sorry. You know I'm on your side. Just be there for her, too. She'll get past it, but it'll take time." It felt weird giving him advice on this, but for some reason, he was convinced this would be easy. "New topic before you go back up the hill," I said. "Is that penny back at your office?"

Dalton rolled in his lips.

"It's still in your pocket, isn't it? It could be worth a million dollars," I reminded him.

He reached in and pulled out the bag containing the penny. "With two murders, I sure hope so."

"I think we should take care of that question once and for all. If you entrust me with it, I'll take it down the hill to Irwin's house. It'll be that second opinion Rusty was after."

Dalton handed it over. "I appreciate the help with this, Scottie. I know this is your day off."

"You know I love a good murder case. Now, go up to the resort. And, remember, put yourself in her six-thousand-dollar leather boots. Like Nana used to tell me—'you don't know anyone until you stand in their shoes.'"

"A wise woman who also makes a perfect stack of pancakes. I think Evie would have been my dream match. Let me know what you find out."

thirty-two

. . .

I WATCHED A CLEARLY distressed man drive off to meet with his even more distressed ex-fiancée. I felt bad that I wasn't being more supportive, but there wasn't any other way to look at it. Clearly, Dalton had convinced himself that Crystal's feelings about him weren't as strong as those she'd had about her wedding. That seemed to be the case when I broke it off with Jonathan. He was far more worried about how canceling the wedding would look to his friends and family than he was heartbroken about losing me. I hoped the two of them could come to terms with this whole mess. Of course, the last thing Dalton needed right now was a double murder. I hoped to ease his burden in that regard. Unfortunately, I was at a loss about who to suspect next. First and foremost, I needed to know once and for all if the penny was genuine or fake. I hoped Nana's old friend, Irwin, could shed some light on the debate.

I drove down the hill and came to a construction crew stop sign. Now that winter was over, there would be a lot of highway work. It was the county's chance to fix whatever damage a long, cold winter had caused.

A man on a giant orange earthmover was plowing up some dirt that had slid down the hillside after the thaw. Once he'd shoveled his load, he spun the vehicle around and headed across the road to the waiting dump truck. The traffic controller spun the sign from stop to slow. I moved past the worksite only to be met with another stop sign just a mile down the hill. This time work crews were working to move a big boulder that had rolled dangerously close to the road. A jackhammer fired up and a big, burly man rammed it against the rock. So far, they'd only made a dent in the boulder. They were going to be at it for hours.

"A jackhammer," I muttered. From the looks of it, the crew had been chiseling away at the rock since early this morning. Dalton and I heard a jackhammer in the background of Daniel's phone call. It was loud enough that Dalton had to pull the phone away from his ear and put it on speaker. There could very well have been a jackhammer making noise near Daniel's office, as he'd explained. The noise stopped and the sign was turned. I drove past the worksite.

The highway motel was just around the bend. It was a small group of rather ramshackle looking cabins tucked under some hundred-foot spruce trees. It certainly didn't look like a place a refined coin expert would be staying. The parking lot was empty except for a bicycle. I was sure Daniel had not made his way up to Ripple Creek on a bike.

I pulled into the parking lot. It was time to put on my best acting skills. I parked in front of the cabin with the office and vacancy signs. The set of cabins were aptly named Spruce Cottages, although *cottage* might have been a stretch. I parked and went into the office. A young man clad in biking gear was sitting behind the front desk watching a mountain bike video on YouTube.

He reluctantly paused the video and stood up to greet me. "I have three cabins left for the night." There were six cabins so that meant three had guests.

"Actually, I was hoping you could help me. I was supposed to meet a friend up here. I wrote down the name of the place we were supposed to meet, but"—I tapped the side of my head—"But I left it on my notepad at home."

"You could have just put it in your phone," he said plainly.

I laughed. "That would have been smart. However, since I didn't do that, I thought I'd stop in here to check. My friend's name is Daniel Lomax."

The clerk eyed me suspiciously. "Is this one of those gotcha things where you're trying to catch your husband in the act?"

I smiled at him. "My generation might be slow on making use of technology, but yours watches far too much reality television." I held up my hand to show him there was no ring. "Daniel is just a friend."

"I guess I can look," he said. He walked over to the computer, hit a few keys and shook his head. "Nope, no Daniel Lomax. Maybe he's up at the resort."

"Right. Maybe so. Thanks for your help." I mustered the

most polite smile I could offer considering the guy was pretty annoying. I headed out to the car just as another car was pulling into the lot. It was Daniel. I ducked down behind my car, so he wouldn't see me. It took him a minute to park. He carried a bag of fast food out from the passenger side and slipped into the third cabin. I heard the office door behind me.

"So, you are following your boyfriend. I thought as much."

My face warmed with a blush as I straightened from my crouch and turned to face him. He was wearing a cocky grin. "What was that about my generation and reality television?"

"Fine. You got me. But you said there was no Daniel Lomax renting a cabin."

"There isn't, but you should get a little more training before you try to do this private eye stuff. People who don't want to be caught in the act rarely check in with their real name."

"And you don't ask for identification?"

He laughed. "Look at this place. It's not exactly the Ritz Carlton. He probably paid in cash. Another thing people do when they don't want to get caught."

I yanked down on the bottom of my coat. "You sure do know a lot about people who don't want to get caught."

He didn't even have the decency to deny it. "For what it's worth, I haven't seen that guy walk in with anyone. Maybe he just needed a break." He punctuated the last word with an arrogant wink before going back into the office.

Daniel was in town. I needed to call Dalton with the news. I got in the car and drove out of the parking lot. I pulled onto the first turnout and picked up my phone. Dalton was in the middle of something heavy, and I hated to bother him, but he needed to know that Daniel Lomax was still on the mountain. But why? Then it occurred to me.

It went straight to voicemail, which wasn't surprising. "Hi, it's me. Guess who is still in town and staying at the Spruce Cottages and a few hundred feet away from a work crew that is jackhammering a boulder? You guessed it. At least, I assume you did. Anyhow, I took a small detour to discover that important nugget of information. Now I'm heading to Irwin's house. I think he'll tell me the penny is real. I hope everything is going all right. Talk to you later."

I hung up and started the car. I was feeling that giddy excitement I always felt whenever I was getting close to solving a murder. I hadn't put all the pieces of the puzzle together yet, but it all had to do with the penny in my purse. I pulled it out to look at it. "Well, Mr. Lincoln, what do you have to say for yourself? You've caused quite a stir in Ripple Creek."

thirty-three

...

IRWIN BABBINGTON LIVED in a small bungalow that was painted butter yellow. There were flower boxes on the windows, but it looked as if it had been some time since they held flowers. I thumbed back through my memory. I was living in the city at the time, but I remember Nana mentioning that she attended Donna Babbington's funeral. It was particularly noteworthy because unbeknownst to the cemetery groundskeeper, a colony of bees had built a hive in the tree above Donna's gravesite, and several of the mourners had walked away with bee stings.

The front windows were crusted with dust. A stream of smoke curled up out of the brick chimney. There was a sign on the door that said no walk-in appraisals. I hoped that Irwin would be willing to help me out. It was important. I was sure, being Evie's granddaughter, he'd be happy to invite me inside.

I stepped on the porch and rang the bell. It clanged somewhere in the back of the house. The door opened. I hadn't seen Irwin in years. He'd aged a great deal since then. His face was mottled with brown age spots, and he looked slighter and shorter than I remembered. His knuckles were big and round as he pulled a pair of eyeglasses up to his face. "No walk-in appraisals." He reached into his shirt pocket and pulled out a card. "Here's my number. Call and make an appointment."

"Actually, Irwin, my name is Scottie. I'm Evie's granddaughter."

He stared at me through cloudy blue eyes "Evie? Is she all right? Has something happened?"

"Evie is fine. I came here because I need an appraisal on a coin."

He shook his head. "Make an appointment."

"But I'm here now," I said quickly as he moved to close the door. "I might have a 1943 Lincoln copper penny." I blurted it before he could shut the door. He pulled it open again and chuckled.

"I'm sorry, dear, but I doubt you have one of those. They are very rare and valuable and unfortunately, there are some impressive fakes floating around. I've got one myself. It was so good, it nearly fooled me." He said the last part with a good dose of pride.

I'd gotten him to reopen the door. Now I needed an invite in for an appraisal. "I remember all the beautiful jewelry you used to make. Are you still making it?"

He squinted his eyes. "Who'd you say you were again?

Oh, that's right. You're little Scottie, Evie's granddaughter. Well, come on inside before you let in the cold air."

The house was warm from the glowing fire. I followed Irwin down a hallway to a room that was lined with cabinets and glass cases. There was a large worktable in the middle of the room, and two pendant lights hung down low from the ceiling.

"Where are my manners?" he asked. "You'll have to excuse me; I don't get many visitors. Would you like a cup of tea?"

"No, I'm fine." I looked around the room. "So, this was where you made all your jewelry?"

"Yep, can't make it anymore. My hands aren't steady enough. But these old eyes still work well enough for appraisals. I've had a lot of interesting jewelry pass under my loupe. Through the years, I've seen it all." He walked to one of the cabinets and pulled out a small drawer. "Now, where is that darn penny?" He adjusted his glasses and searched through some coins. "Aha, here it is. About ten years back a man came to me, beside himself with excitement, sure that he'd found a 1943 Lincoln copper penny. He was so happy, I almost hated to tell him it was a fake." Irwin carried the coin over to the table. He pointed at one of the stools, and I sat down. He lowered the pendant light much like a dentist might pull a light down over his patient. His fingers were shaky for a second, but as soon as he held the coin's edge pinched between his fingers, his hand stilled. He picked up his loupe and held it over the coin. "Take a close look at the three on the date."

I leaned over the loupe and stared down at the magnified date. "It looks like a three."

"It does. Only if you look very closely you can see the small dent on the top curve of the three. That's because it was a seven before the counterfeiter changed it into a three. They did an impressive job. It took me a few minutes to notice that the top of the three was just a hair too flat. For a brief moment, I thought I was holding a genuine 1943 copper penny in my hand. The poor man was devastated when I told him. He didn't want to believe me at first. I told him to take it to another appraiser just to be sure, but he decided not to. He left the penny. I kept it as a reminder of how good these fakes can be."

I leaned over and looked through the loupe again. "Now that you've pointed out the flaw, I can see it. Like you said, it's just a hair too flat." I reached into my pocket and pulled out the baggie with the coin.

"That looks like an evidence bag," Irwin said.

"Yes, I'm afraid this penny has caused two people to be murdered."

Irwin shook his head. "And it's probably just a worthless piece of metal." He took the coin from the bag and checked it with a magnet. "Well, it passed the first test. A fake would stick to the magnet." He pulled out his loupe. He turned the coin over on his palm a few times feeling the weight of it, then he got down to business. He scrutinized every detail, taking his time and even lowering the pendant light a few times for a better view. At one point, he put down the penny and got up. He paced from one side of the room to the other, scratching his chin in thought. Without another word, he sat back down and examined the coin again. "Well, I'll be. I've only ever seen one of these at an auction. It sold for nine-hundred-thousand dollars."

"So, it's real?" I asked. I'd been driving around with a million bucks in my purse.

"As far as I'm concerned, that is a genuine 1943 Lincoln copper penny. And it's a nice one. That'd catch a fair price at auction. Is that who was murdered? The owner of that coin?"

"There's been a good deal of controversy about who actually owns the coin, but to answer your question, yes, the man who found the penny is dead. His friend is, too. You might know them—Rusty Simmer and Cameron Burke." I hated to blurt the names so plainly, but I saw no other way to do it.

"I've spoken to them at coin collector meetings. Both nice people. What a shame."

"Cameron brought an appraiser up to Ripple Creek to authenticate that penny, but Daniel said it was a fake."

Irwin's eyes rounded behind his lenses. "Daniel? Not Daniel Lomax?"

"Yes, that's the man."

Irwin shook his head. "No, no, Lomax cannot be trusted. Oh, he knows his stuff well enough, but he uses his expertise to cheat people out of their valuables. He's notorious for telling people something is worth less than its true value. Then he buys it off them for a slightly higher value, and they're happy to take the offer. If he said this was a fake, then he was up to his usual shenanigans." Irwin's face lost some color. "But if the police are in possession of the coin, that means his plan failed. Maybe he took his usual scam even farther. My goodness, did Daniel Lomax kill those two men?"

"That's the question of the day, Irwin."

Irwin placed the penny back into the evidence bag and held it up. "Thank you so much for bringing this here. I've had plenty of fakes come through, but it's nice to finally see the real thing. Be careful with it," he said as he handed me the bag.

"I will keep it tucked inside my pocket until I get it back to the police."

"Where is Lomax now?" Irwin asked.

"I think he's staying close to Ripple Creek. Cameron came to see me just before he was murdered. He said he had something important to tell me. I think Cameron found the penny in Daniel's belongings. He must have suspected that Daniel was up to something. Cameron had it hidden in the back of his television remote. I happened upon it when I was helping Ranger Braddock search Cameron's house for evidence."

Irwin grinned. "Then it sounds like you're the new owner of the penny. You'll be rich."

"Yes, well, I'll be handing it over to the police, and they can decide where it should go next."

He chuckled. "You don't need a million dollars?"

I smiled. "I really appreciate you taking the time to look at the penny." I got up from the stool.

"It was my pleasure. I'm only sorry two people had to die over that coin. I hope they catch Daniel Lomax. His trip to jail has been a long time coming."

Catching Daniel was next on my agenda, but how? Then a

brilliant idea popped into my head, impressive considering the weekend I'd been having. "Irwin, would you mind if I borrowed that fake coin for a day? I can bring it right back."

"Go ahead." His smile caused a whole group of lines to appear on his cheeks. "Are you going to lure the snake out with the fake?"

"That's exactly what I'm going to do."

thirty-four

• • •

MORE OF MY brilliant plan came together as I drove back up to Ripple Creek. I passed the Spruce Cottages. Daniel's car was still parked in the lot, and the work crew was still hammering the boulder into manageable chunks. A big realization popped into my head while I waited for the stop sign to change. If Daniel Lomax killed Rusty and Cameron, why was he still in town? That answer was easy. He didn't want to leave without the coin. He knew all along that he'd been looking at the real thing. But his plan went awry when Rusty decided to hold onto the coin and get a second opinion. Daniel knew that Rusty would then learn he had a real 1943 Lincoln copper penny, and Daniel would lose out on his chance at a million-dollar payout.

The man holding the sign was waving anxiously for me to move. I'd gotten so lost in my thoughts I hadn't noticed the sign change. I drove up the highway. As far as Daniel knew, the penny was still in Cameron's house. He'd given it a good once-over, but something must have panicked him, so he left without the coin. He'd taken a room nearby because he planned to go back for it. After all, he'd committed two heinous crimes for that penny.

I reached Cameron's street. I glanced at my phone. No message from Dalton. His day was not going nearly as well as mine. I was so close to wrapping this thing up, I felt like a million bucks. Of course, the fact that I had the penny in my pocket probably helped. I decided not to take any chances with the real coin. I opened the glove box, took out my car registration and slipped the coin, baggie and all, into the sleeve. I shut the glove box. I pulled the fake coin out of my pocket and grabbed my phone.

Yellow caution tape was draped between the two porch posts. The front door was still broken, so it opened easily. I walked straight to the far bedroom. The bed linens were rumpled, and the closet door was open. It was empty. This was Cameron's guest bedroom. It hadn't been torn apart like the rest of the house. That made sense. Daniel was probably staying in the room, so it was the one place he could skip in his search.

I stepped into the hallway. A shiver ran through me. A man had just been murdered in the house, and it was still in a violent state of mess. Someone had swept up the broken glass in the kitchen. Presumably, the shards had been sent to forensics for tests. A light chalk outline on the kitchen floor showed the exact location where Cameron collapsed to his death.

I needed to make this as easy as possible for Daniel without it seeming like an obvious sting operation. There went another shiver, only this time it was because I was excited to participate in my first sting.

It was time to plant the lure, as Irwin had so aptly called it. I glanced around the front room. It needed to be hidden in plain sight. It occurred to me then that I, too, needed to be hidden but less in plain sight because I definitely didn't want to be discovered. Daniel had killed two men in cold blood. I doubted he'd let me stand in his way.

Cameron's front room was small and squeezed tight with furniture. I moved into the kitchen, the scene of the crime, so to speak. Drawers hung open and seemingly everything had been turned inside out. Then I spotted something, something funny and round and seemingly untouched in all the chaos. It was a cookie jar in the shape of a fat, smiling rabbit. I walked over and pulled on the big ears. The entire smiling head popped off. There were a few sandwich cookies in the bottom of the jar. I dropped in the penny and then left the head just a tiny bit askew to catch Daniel's attention. It was entirely possible he'd looked inside the jar in his earlier hunt, but it seemed odd that he'd have taken the time to replace the top given the state of the rest of the kitchen. The door on the broom closet hung open, much like all the other doors in the house. The brooms, mop and buckets had been conveniently cleared out. They were strewn around the floor. I stepped carefully over the mess and slipped into the closet. It was dark, but there was plenty of room for me—the stinger. I closed the door but left it slightly ajar, open enough that I could record Daniel's movements with my phone. Now all I had to do was wait—always the boring part of a sting operation.

Fortunately for this *stinger*, Daniel Lomax arrived just ten minutes later. He walked brazenly in the front door, right past the caution tape that was there because he committed murder inside the house. Admittedly, my stalwart resolve to catch him in the act had crumpled some. Hearing his footsteps gave me a good dose of nerves. I could hear my own pulse as I stood silently inside the broom closet. I took a few deep, quiet breaths to steady myself.

Daniel threw things around in the front room. He growled out cuss words as he rummaged through the few items he hadn't already torn apart in the house. His plodding footsteps echoed down the hallway as he stretched his search to the bedrooms and bathroom.

I was feeling plenty nervous, but at the same time, I knew I had this. When his irritated footsteps reached the kitchen, I held up my phone, aimed it at the cookie jar and pressed record. For a smart man, it sure took him a long time to realize the cookie jar lid was crooked. He marched across the floor and yanked the jar across the counter. He pulled off the head and tossed it behind him on the floor. The ears broke off, but the bunny was still smiling as the head rolled toward the closet door. Daniel dumped the cookies out on the counter, and the penny landed on the tile.

"There you are, *my pretty*." He even said it in the famous Wicked Witch tone.

I had it all on tape. After Daniel left, I'd find Dalton and show him the evidence. My sting operation was going beautifully...until my phone rang. Rookie mistake, as they say.

Daniel shoved the penny into his pocket as his face snapped in the direction of the broom closet. "Who's there?"

I had no chance to check the screen. I only hoped it was Dalton getting back to me. I flicked my thumb over the screen to answer and then stuck the phone in my pocket. I stepped out of the closet.

"What are you doing here?" Daniel barked.

"I should ask what you are doing here in *Cameron's house*?"

"You first. You're that baker. I thought you were awfully nosy. Well, I just came in to find my watch. I forgot it. Too bad about Cameron. He was a nice guy." He turned to leave. I should have been relieved that he was going, but the sleuth in me said not so fast.

"You killed Rusty so you could steal the penny," I said. He stopped and turned around. "I know it's real. Rusty knew that, too. That's why he kept it."

"The fool should have taken my word for it."

"Except you were lying. But then lying is the way you do business, isn't it? Then Cameron discovered that you had the penny," I said.

"He must have seen me admiring it. He stole it from me when I wasn't looking. That coin should never have ended up here in this stupid little town. It belongs with me." He patted his pocket. "I've finally found my holy grail, the coin that will make me rich and famous in the collector's world."

"The only place you'll be famous is in jail when the other inmates find out you killed two men over a penny." I knew I was pushing my luck, but I hoped I could stall him long enough with conversation. Then a horrid thought occurred to me. What if Dalton was miles away?

Daniel's expression turned dark and angry. He moved toward me. "I suppose I'll have to take care of the one person who figured this out. I already killed two people. One more isn't going to make any difference to me." He moved toward me; his hands cupped together as if ready to grab my throat.

"Too bad you don't have the real coin," I blurted.

Daniel stopped a few feet away and squeezed his face together in doubt. "You're lying."

"I'm not."

He pulled the coin out and held it up to the light coming through the window. It was my chance. I rammed into him and knocked him off balance. He was fast. He grabbed my arm and yanked it painfully behind my back. "If you know this one is a fake, then you must know where the real one is."

"I do, but I can't tell you if I'm dead." My heart was pounding, and my shoulder and arm ached from the way he was holding me.

"Show me," he growled in my ear.

"Front room." He kept tight hold of my arm and pushed me forward toward the front room. We reached the television.

"Cameron told me he hid it under the back of the television."

He pushed me forward. "You find it. I'll be right behind you."

I'd gotten myself into a pickle. I knew too well that the real penny was in my glove box and not under the television.

I leaned forward and reached around the side of the television. I made a good show of searching blindly, all the while trying to plan my next move. I was about to kick out and hope my foot landed hard on something painful when I heard a groan followed by a thud. I straightened and spun around. Daniel was crumpled on the ground. Cade stood behind him rubbing his fist.

"That hurt more than I expected. I'm guess I'm not well equipped for knocking people senseless."

Daniel was just starting to come around. I looked up at Cade. "I don't know about that. I think you did a pretty good job."

"The killer, I presume?" Cade asked.

"Indeed." I pulled the phone out of my pocket. "So that was you on the other end. How did you find me?"

"I was on a walk, and I spotted your car. You didn't answer my call, and since I know your propensity for getting into trouble, I thought I'd check on you."

Dalton pulled up out front.

"Ah, the official has arrived. I suppose that's my cue to leave." Cade turned back to me. "You gave me quite the scare, Ramone."

"I'm sorry. But thank you for coming so fast."

Cade nodded. "My pleasure."

thirty-five

. . .

I CARRIED the nice bottle of wine up to Cade's door. The two men had been more civil than usual after I'd explained everything to Dalton. Dalton actually thanked Cade for stepping in to protect me. That was as far as the exchange had gone. Dalton had an arrest to make, and Cade made a quick exit. I did, too. The excitement of my big sting operation had exhausted me.

Cade pulled open the door before I could knock. I handed him the wine. "It's supposed to be a good one. I wanted to say thank you for this afternoon."

He nodded for me to come in. "I'm glad you're here. I need to talk to you."

"If this is still about the kiss, I liked everything about it, Cade, so stop second guessing yourself."

Cade carried the wine into the kitchen and pulled out the corkscrew. "Dalton broke up with Crystal," he blurted.

I stared at him. "That certainly came out of left field."

"I heard it when I was buying peanut butter and bread at the market. I learn so much when I'm at that market. You knew, of course." There was almost accusation in his tone.

"Yes, he told me. But that has nothing to do with us."

His jaw looked tight as he poured the wine. Our fingers grazed each other as he handed me the glass. "No, it has nothing to do with *us*, but it has everything to do with you."

"It really doesn't." I sounded less than convincing. "More than anything, I need to focus on my business."

Cade nodded. "Interesting way of telling me we're never going to be a thing."

"Not true. I'm just so busy with work, I'm worried a relationship will get in the way. But, Cade, I don't want us to stop seeing each other. I enjoy being with you."

"And I enjoy being with you, Ramone. I also think a little time apart won't hurt. It'll help us clear our heads."

"What do you mean?" I asked. "Are you leaving?"

He took a sip of wine. "Oh, that is a good one. My publisher is insisting I go on a book tour in Europe. My latest book is just hitting bookstores there."

I raised a skeptical brow. "Your publisher?"

"Yes, truly. I admit I don't mind the idea of spending some time in Europe."

His news was hitting me harder than I expected. I didn't want him to go. "How long?" I asked airily, as if it didn't matter. Only it seemed to matter a lot. My limbs felt heavy just thinking about it.

"Just four weeks or so. No definitive return date yet."

"That sounds open-ended and—" I gazed at him. "You *will* come back, Cade?"

He put down the glass of wine and walked over to me. He took the glass from my hand and pulled me into his arms. No kiss. Just a hug that I realized right then I desperately needed.

"Yes, I will come back," Cade said.

I leaned back and peered up at him. I knew my expression was packed with emotion because I could feel that same emotion through my entire body.

Cade reached up and lightly brushed a strand of hair from my forehead. "I'll be back, Ramone. I promise."

thirty-six

...

ONCE I ABSORBED the news that Cade was leaving on a book tour and we both managed to pull ourselves out of the funk his departure and my wishy-washy insecurities had caused, Cade and I had a nice evening. The wine was good, and the conversation was even better. It had been a long day and after my third yawn, Cade walked me to the car. He kissed me on the forehead. He'd be leaving for Europe in a week. With any luck, he'd be back just in time for summer.

I pulled up to Nana's house and was somehow not surprised to find Dalton sitting on the front porch.

"I don't see your truck," I said.

"No, I walked here. I needed the exercise and the cool night air." He stood up from the step. I sensed he had something to tell me.

He came down the steps to meet me. We stopped in front of each other. We'd never kissed, and yet, somehow, it felt like we had. There was a connection that I could only describe as profound. But I found out tonight, when Cade bluntly delivered the news that he was leaving, that I had a profound connection with him as well.

Dalton took my hand. "First of all, thank you for your help." He chuckled lightly. "Help," he repeated. "It was more than that. You singlehandedly solved the case. I know this sounds strange coming out of *my* mouth, but I'm glad Rafferty was there. Lomax is a dangerous man. He was not going to leave town without that penny. Lomax confessed everything. Cameron had pointed out Henry's house as they drove past earlier in the day. On his way to Rusty's, Daniel spotted the Voight's open garage and couldn't pass up the opportunity to frame Henry. What he hadn't counted on was Scottie Ramone solving the case."

"What will happen with the penny?" I asked.

"Not sure. A lawyer for the county said it could be sold first to pay for the funerals of the two men. They are going to bring Henry and Amy in for a meeting to talk about ownership and sharing the rest."

"They'll both be so happy. I only wish Rusty hadn't died before he found out the truth about his coin." I looked up at him. "Second of all?"

Dalton's forehead bunched.

"You started with first of all, so I figured there was a second of all." I pressed my hand against his mouth before he could answer. "You and Crystal are going to work things out."

His face dropped, and he took hold of my hand. "She's a

mess. I had no idea she'd react like this. She's agreed to postpone the wedding for now."

"Is that possible?" I asked.

"It is when you're a Miramont. But if I'm being honest, I don't see any chance of pulling this back together."

I patted his hand with my free hand. "You may end up surprising yourself. And in the meantime—"

"You'll wait for me?" he asked anxiously.

"In the meantime, I've got a bakery to run. You've got your life, and I've got mine. I think it's best if we focus on that for now. Don't forget, your happiness is as important as hers," I reminded him.

"And that's the piece that has me doubting the whole thing."

Dalton moved closer. "We're still friends, right? I can't go through this without your support."

"We're still friends. Just don't tell Crystal." I stepped into his arms for a hug and instantly found myself trying to compare it to Cade's hug. This was so crazy. How could it feel so right to be standing in Cade's arms and then have it feel exactly right in Dalton's embrace? What a mess. I needed to stick to brownies and cupcakes.

about the author

London Lovett is the author of the Port Danby, Starfire, Firefly Junction, Scottie Ramone and Frostfall Island Cozy Mystery series. She loves getting caught up in a good mystery and baking delicious, new treats!

Learn more at:
www.londonlovett.com

Printed in Great Britain
by Amazon